BRUTAL OBSESSION

The Safeguard Series, Book One

Kennedy Layne

BRUTAL OBSESSION

Copyright © 2016 by Kennedy Layne
Print Edition

E-Book ISBN: 978-1-943420-10-0
Print ISBN: 978-1-682303-64-1

Cover Design: Sweet 'N Spicy Designs

Dedication

Jeffrey—it just keeps getting better and better…I love you!

Lisa—I cannot thank you enough for the gift card to Starbucks! Deadlines aren't so bad when a cup of coffee is in hand!

From USA Today Bestselling Author Kennedy Layne comes a thrilling new military romantic suspense series that will leave you on the edge of your seat...

Keane Sanderson never thought he'd survive to see a day past his latest deployment with the United States Marines in Iraq. That was six years ago and he's finally ready to ease off the accelerator. A unique opportunity to work for a top-shelf security and investigations firm in Florida is right up his alley.

Ashlyn Ellis had everything she'd ever wanted—a high-profile career as a federal prosecutor, an upscale apartment in the city, and a beach house for when she needed to decompress from all the stress that accompanied the job. All three are threatened when she realizes someone has been following her every move for a very long time.

When Ashlyn comprehends the lengths her pursuer is willing to take things, she calls in a favor. She never expected her plea for assistance to materialize in the form of Keane Sanderson—the one man who had every reason to revel in her misfortune. She's finally given the chance to rekindle the flames of desire she never should have extinguished, just in time for it all to be taken away when the stalker takes his obsession a step too far.

CHAPTER ONE

THE EVENLY SPACED, razor-edged shafts of moonlight fragmented the heavy darkness. The shimmering beams were mesmerizing as they peered through the wooden slats of the shutters, allowing a few dust particles to twirl through the rays as if they were performing on a lighted stage. It was a captivating sight and one that gave her something to do other than stress over the insomnia that had plagued her for the last few months.

Ashlyn Ellis sighed in resignation as she shifted beneath the warm, crumpled sheets. She'd woken up five minutes ago, noticing that she'd gotten no more than three hours of sleep according to the green illuminated numbers of the clock on her nightstand. She tucked an arm under her favorite Hungarian goose down pillow in frustration after turning on her side, but not even the cool eight hundred count Egyptian fabric could lull her into a comforting sleep. It was an hour before dawn and the rhythmic ticking of the grandfather clock in the living room was the only sound drifting through the still air. Or was it?

Click.

Ashlyn's breath caught in her throat as she quickly leaned up on one elbow and tilted her head, straining to hear if there were any unwelcome sounds coming from the hidden recesses of the

KENNEDY LAYNE

bottomless shadows. Had she been mistaken? The air was now
frozen in place as the golden pendulum continued to swing with
a graceful cadence, but the stillness had undeniably been
disturbed.

Was *he* here?

Ashlyn slowly leaned forward and carefully opened the top
drawer of her bedside table, never once taking her eyes away
from the open door to her bedroom. Multiple shadows hovered
at the end of the hall, appearing slightly darker than usual due to
the soft golden hue of the nightlight plugged into the outlet. Her
fingers finally came in contact with her nickel-plated Beretta
PX4 Storm Subcompact handgun. It gave her a small semblance
of security.

A slight film of perspiration coated Ashlyn's palm, making it
difficult to maintain a grip on the mother of pearl handgrip of
the weapon. She still managed to aim the barrel toward the
hallway as she slid the covers off and quietly swung her legs over
the side of her bed. Had the shadow to the right shifted
somewhat lower?

Ashlyn carefully felt around the top of her nightstand for her
phone, not wanting to make any loud noises. Was he watching
her? Was he standing at the end of the hall, waiting for her to
think she had a chance of calling for help before making his
move? Was he here to finally kill her?

There was no phone on her bedside table. Her heart rate
accelerated even more at the implication and she tried to stem
her panic. Where was it? Had he been standing next to her bed
and watching her sleep? She tried to swallow the revulsion that
backed up in her throat.

Ashlyn glanced down to the floor, thinking her phone had
possibly fallen. It was only then she remembered leaving it in her
office on its charging stand, which was on the other side of her

apartment. She didn't have a landline in her home and her security system linked through an independent cellular data plan, which apparently hadn't done its job. How was she going to get help now?

Nausea slammed into Ashlyn and she pursed her lips, doing her best to breathe through her panic. She stood on slightly trembling legs, her bare feet cold on the hardwood floor. The shocking sensation gave her a sense of foundation and she took a tentative step forward, needing to get to her office. Why couldn't she hear him? What was he waiting for?

Ashlyn passed by her mirrored dresser on her left, almost letting out a small cry when she caught her silhouette in the reflection. She took a moment to calm her racing heart. It was then she noticed that the drawer holding her panties had been left slightly open…and she hadn't left it that way after her evening shower. He'd gone through her things…her intimate belongings?

He *was* here.

She swallowed against the queasiness as she contemplated flipping the switch beside the doorframe, but that meant releasing one of her hands from the only protection she had and alerting anyone in the apartment that she was awake. She refused to do that and forced herself to move forward.

Ashlyn's upper body began to hurt from the way her heart was slamming against her chest. She considered herself a strong woman, but this constant fear she'd been living in these last few months had taken its toll. It had definitely put a few dents in her armor and her resolution to continue living as if *he* wasn't a real threat to her safety. He'd just proved her wrong. She didn't like being made a fool of and tried to find her justifiable anger, but it was buried too deep under the fear he'd instilled in her.

"I'm armed and I will shoot," Ashlyn called out, wincing at

the tremor in her tone that suggested she was absolutely terrified. She was, but she didn't need to announce that fact. She took another tentative step and managed to continue until she reached the end of the hallway, holding her weapon as steady as she could. "I won't miss either."

Why wasn't he answering? Was this what he wanted?

Ashlyn reached the end of the hallway. She looked everywhere, grateful she'd left the light on underneath the over-the-range microwave oven. Nothing appeared out of place and no one was in sight. She had an open layout, so she quickly scanned it once more, taking in as many details as she could.

Where was he?

Ashlyn wasn't sure she could hear him over her uneven breathing, so she held her breath while skimming her gaze over anyplace he could be hiding. Was he behind the large arch that separated the kitchen from the living room? Was he hiding behind the couch? What about the long Parisian Fall curtains that covered the double windows overlooking the Capitol? She slowly exhaled, unable to stop her unnerved senses from believing something was still amiss.

The front door was to Ashlyn's left. It was located in a very small foyer that was beside the entrance to the kitchen. She shot a glance toward her office, wanting to get to her cell phone, but she figured she had a better chance of getting to safety if she ran out into the hallway and sought help from one of her neighbors. Would he finally show himself if she made a run for it?

She sidestepped, never once taking her gaze away from the living room. She calculated she was still ten feet away from the door when the corner of the thin Edwardian style entryway table dug into her upper thigh. She bit the side of her lip to prevent herself from crying out when the Venetian crystal vase wobbled and eventually fell to the floor with a loud, reverberating crash.

Ashlyn cringed and braced herself for the inevitable attack. It never came. The high-pitched noise from the shattered glass reverberated in her ears, but her chance of freedom was now or never. She ran as fast as she could, skipping over the shards of glass as best she could, finally releasing one of her hands from her handgun to open the door…only to find that it was secure.

That couldn't be right.

Ashlyn quickly glanced over her shoulder to make sure he wasn't behind her as she continued to try to turn the doorknob. It wouldn't budge. She ran a hand up to the deadbolt, only to find it bolted shut. It made no sense and yet she couldn't feel his presence now that her sanity slowly returned.

The light switch was next to the front closet, so Ashlyn reached out and flipped it up while spinning around to face her apartment. She brought her weapon even with her gaze while taking a shaky breath as anger finally started to shove away the deep-seated fear.

That was what he truly wanted—her fear.

Ashlyn slowly crossed the hardwood floor onto the kitchen slate, moving sideways so that she could still maintain a view of the entire area. She continued to turn on every light as she made her way out of the kitchen, through the small dining room and into her home office. It seemed to take her an hour, but it couldn't have been more than a minute or two.

A bubbling, hysterical laugh tried to come out when Ashlyn realized no one was there. She cautiously looked down at her modern glass and steel desk, seeing her cell phone positioned exactly where she'd left it on the small round charger connected to her computer. She walked around her desk, keeping a watchful eye on the apartment laid out before her as she reached for the device, now second-guessing placing a 911 call when there was no evidence of foul play. Either they wouldn't believe her, just sending a cruiser through the area, or they'd simply file a report after talking her down. She knew the justice system well.

Had she been the one to leave her dresser drawer open when she got ready for bed? He had her second-guessing herself, just as he had all along.

Ashlyn took a step toward the door only to immediately stop when a sharp pain radiated through the heel of her foot. She lifted up her leg and hopped back, leaning against her desk. She was bleeding. A shard of glass was embedded in her left foot and she'd trailed blood throughout her apartment all over the Mazama hardwood she'd handpicked upon moving to Washington D.C and finding the right apartment that fit her eclectic style.

The wheels of the black leather chair rolled back when Ashlyn sat down, her adrenaline finally fading as the pain took hold. Tears stung her eyes as exhaustion settled over her. She couldn't keep going on like this. She was so worn out from the constant fear and she was coming to the realization that she needed to do something about it. She needed to take control, but unfortunately she wasn't sure from whom.

Ashlyn reached out for a tissue in the box she always kept on her desk when something caught her eye. She stopped in mid-motion, her arm hovering above her desk. No. That couldn't be right. She stared at the steady green light on top of her monitor as the significance of what she was seeing weighed down on her, causing the pain in her foot to momentarily disappear.

He was playing with her.

He was watching her.

Ashlyn now had no doubt left that he'd been in her apartment tonight. Revulsion hit her hard, but she was tired…so tired of being scared. A calculating coldness finally settled in and she purposefully smiled as she leaned back against her chair. She never once wavered her steady gaze as she dialed 911 and lifted the phone to her ear.

"I'd like to report a break-in," Ashlyn said in a controlled manner when the 911 operator inquired about her problem. Was he listening? She leaned closer so that he couldn't mistake the challenge in her eyes or the words that passed her lips. "Please send a unit to…"

Piercing pain made itself known when Ashlyn tried to place her left foot on the floor as she rattled off her address. She wouldn't show her discomfort to the man who was watching her. She refused and sat up a little straighter.

"My name?" Ashlyn tilted her head and leveled a look at the camera as if she were looking at a defendant in court. She made a promise to herself that one of these days he would be. "Federal Prosecutor Ashlyn Ellis."

HIS HEART RATE stuttered when Ashlyn leaned into the camera, her blue eyes staring directly into his imprisoned soul.

Did she feel it like he did?

Did she feel their ethereal connection?

There were times when he would swear that he could actually see the gossamer thread that connected her spirit to his when they were close. He slowly raised a hand and then lightly traced her face on one of the monitors he'd dedicated to watching the feed from her laptop camera full time, not stopping until he'd circled her full lips completely. Even after her evening shower, they still managed to hold a lighter shade of the lipstick she'd worn earlier today.

He routinely recorded the footage he got from her computer's camera and then edited out the times when she wasn't in-frame. It cost him several hours a night to catalog the digital images of her pristine visage. It was all worth the occasional video capture of her at home in minimal clothing, relaxing as if she didn't know he was there to see her.

He wondered if her lips were as soft as they appeared.

Would they taste like the coffee she drank every morning?

He couldn't prevent himself from leaning forward and pressing his lips against the warm screen as he touched himself.

She would forever be his.

"Please send a unit to…"

Did she really think that the police could keep them apart? Did she think he was a complete idiot? He was smarter than all of those would-be Sam Spade types. The spike of anger hit him directly in the chest and he curled his lips in disgust at her meager attempt to pull someone else into their relationship.

She was his gift, given to him for his faithful obedience to the word. Did she need for him to prove himself once again? Did she want him to show her just how strong of a mate he was for her?

Was what he had already done not good enough for her?

He abruptly stood as she rattled off her address, dropping the lace underwear he'd been holding in his sweaty hand to his cluttered secondhand desk.

He couldn't breathe. Her words reverberated through the small room as he punched his forehead over and over to remove the pain. It didn't prevent her from giving the 911 operator the rest of her information.

What had the psychiatrist said to do when he could sense he was losing control of his violent temper? That's right. Start counting to ten while thinking of something more pleasant—like her body asleep before him when he visited at night. He deliberately tore his eyes from the screen in the attempt to seek out the only thing in his apartment to give him comfort.

There. The rage inside of him gradually eased until even his fists loosened, eventually relaxing enough to pick up the bottom half of Ashlyn's lingerie. He reassured himself that he'd have the other half as soon as she'd worn it.

"My name?"

He spoke his surname over hers as she stated the information.

It sounded like music to his ears.

She was his gift.

CHAPTER TWO

K EANE SANDERSON CONTINUED to drive down the gravel lane lined with old growth American Elms, their abundant green leaves providing shade for the arrow-straight journey that seemed to take longer than necessary. The fully-grown trees had to have been planted over a hundred years ago to acquire such hefty size and such an extensive network of branches reaching out for the heavens.

The texture of the thick bark was impressive and could no doubt withstand whatever severe weather was brought their way. He was envious of the history they'd been around to experience. He only hoped that the trees would continue to escape the ravages of the elm disease that had plagued so many of their brethren in this part of the country.

The ringing of Keane's cell phone cut through the peaceful excursion he'd been about to make to visit with his new employer. He grimaced at the intrusion and reached for his cell phone he'd placed in the center console of the mid-sized American sedan that he'd rented. It wasn't his preferred method of traveling, but it would do until he'd finished his move to the Sunshine State next month.

Sadie.

The name appearing on the display made it rather hard to

ignore the plea. Rather than continue on and be forced to cut a conversation with his sister short, he slowed down and pulled off to the side of the lane. He shifted into park, but allowed the engine to idle as he swiped to accept the call on the small screen.

"Sadie," Keane answered, already knowing why his sister was calling this early in the morning. She should have already started her shift at the hospital. "I've got one minute before I need to go into a meeting."

"Did you know?" Sadie demanded in a heated manner, not bothering with pleasantries. She always did like to put up a front, but he could hear the hurt lacing her tone. "Dad cannot sell the house, Keane. Mom wouldn't have wanted him to either. He'd be giving up so much, not to mention his beloved workshop out back. It's what keeps him sane after all that has happened. You need to talk some sense into him, because we all know he won't listen to me."

Keane leaned an arm out the window as Sadie continued on about why their father selling their sprawling childhood home wasn't a good idea. He understood her reluctance, but their mother had been gone for over three years now. It was time for Don Sanderson to move on and Keane understood he couldn't do that with all of those memories packed between those four walls.

"Sadie," Keane cut in gently, "it's time."

"No, it's not—"

"Yes, it is." Keane surveyed the immediate area as he took time to explain why their father was ready to live life again. "Dad retired a year ago and what does he do besides bounce around inside that place like a frozen pea in a boxcar? He spends his days out back in the workshop and rarely leaves that huge house. He's become stagnant at the age of sixty-seven. He wants to travel, visit you up in Seattle and me down here in Florida, and go to all of the places he's talked about since we were kids. Selling the house isn't selling our memories, Sadie. It's just too much for him to keep up with. He's paying a cleaning service to dust rooms weekly that he never uses."

The long pause on the line had Keane knowing he'd gotten through to his sister. She'd eventually come around to the idea that their father had a life to lead and they couldn't be his personal advisors with such a biased position. Don Sanderson was his own navigator, ready to set sail for something more than mundane days and lonely nights roaming the empty halls of his legacy.

Keane was waiting for Sadie to reply when the breeze picked up, revealing something that really didn't come as a surprise. He never would have noticed it had he not been trying to look at the clouds through the leaves for the thunderstorms the weatherman had spoken of this morning.

High up in the elm tree directly to his left was a surveillance camera, hidden discreetly on one of the higher branches. He didn't doubt it was one of many. His new employer was a start-up security and investigations firm, and the sole owner was known for his penchant for reconnaissance technology. Word on the street was that there was a private backer, but no one could confirm that piece of information when Keane had tried to do some research after receiving the job offer.

"I hate you."

"No, you don't," Keane argued affectionately as he lifted a hand of acknowledgement toward the camera. He had most likely been monitored the moment he'd taken a left on this private drive. "You love me. You only hate the fact that I'm moving to Florida and that you can no longer vet any woman I decide to take to dinner and a movie."

"Please. You're so full of yourself," Sadie replied, a smile finally forming in her voice. "You don't take women to dinner. You take them into your bed, make them breakfast after the fact, and then kick them out before they can ask you your last name."

Keane was well aware that his only healthy relationship with a member of the female persuasion was with his sister. His time in the United States Marine Corps hadn't been well-suited for a stable relationship. He'd tried once, when he'd fulfilled his third contract after twelve years, but that particular woman had gone to great lengths to point out why he wasn't cut out for civilian life or a meaningful relationship. Her speech had left somewhat of an impression.

"Damn, I have to go," Sadie exclaimed over the sounds of high-pitched beeping and the muffled voices of her co-workers. "I still think Dad should keep the house, but I'll ease up on him. Maybe I'll buy it myself and relive my youth. Good luck. Love you. Bye."

Before Keane could respond to any of what Sadie had just said, she'd hung up and disconnected the line. He shook his head at the speed in which his sister lived her life, as well as threw out her thoughts, wishing he could teach her to slow down and enjoy the time they'd been given. Every day was a good day that someone wasn't shooting at you. At least, that was what he told himself and he was rarely disappointed.

Wasn't that why he'd resigned from the LAPD SWAT? Keane had been in enough harrowing situations, throughout his military career and that of his subsequent civilian career, to know when to hang up his hat. This move to a higher-end investigation firm on a smaller scale was his fresh start, but the amount of surveillance on this vast acreage had him wondering if something hadn't been left out of the welcome aboard package.

Keane set his cell phone back into the console before shifting the sedan back into gear. He pressed the accelerator and slowly navigated the rest of the private drive until it opened up into a clearing that revealed quite a shock.

Instead of the usual Floridian housing structures that were so common, a large modern log cabin was positioned among the sheltering shade trees with not a pine tree in sight. Why would someone move to Florida, open a business in the Sunshine State, and *not* live the dream of the typical plantation house on a property of this size?

A large pond, almost big enough to be classified as a lake, could be seen behind the property. It was the detached log outbuilding that caught Keane's attention. It could technically be used as a security post this far out from the main entrance. It wouldn't surprise him after what he'd seen on his way in.

The deep colors of the naturally aged oak matched the main house. Speaking of which, the place had to be north of six thousand square feet, not including the attached four door garage.

There appeared to be quarters over the garage from the look of the dormers, which should be letting in plenty of light. Defending the grounds in a firefight would prove to be easy and it left Keane wondering if that had been a consideration in planning the layout. The massive oak logs could stop a .50 caliber round if they had to. Somebody had put some money into this venture and he was beginning to second-guess his initial impressions of his new employer.

The double doors opening into one of the garage bays were standing wide open and a custom painted silver 2002 VRSC V-Rod Harley Davidson could be seen inside, challenging the apparent tranquil lifestyle created here. Keane could hear the ratcheting brass notes of Wagner's classical *Ride of the Valkyries* drifting from inside after he'd shut off his engine. It was then that Keane caught sight of the contradicting man himself.

Townes Calvert.

Owner and operator of Safeguard Security & Investigations (SSI).

A retired Gunnery Sergeant for the United States Marines.

Keane only had the pleasure of meeting the man once in California when they'd met up for drinks. Calvert had a rough edge to him, but so did a lot of men in this business. He'd presented himself well, wearing khakis and a buttoned down shirt with pressed creases in all the right places. Still, Calvert appeared to buck the system with his long, dark hair pulled back into a ponytail at the base of his neck, which did have a black eagle, globe, and anchor tattoo inked into his tanned skin.

The broken nose added character to Calvert's face, although Keane doubted the women thought him too attractive. He looked as if he'd spent a few rounds in the ring with Muhammad Ali while in his prime.

Regardless, the man had a reputation of being solid and the opportunity to work for him came highly recommended by a couple of Keane's old contacts from his military days. This was the change he'd been looking for…a calmer life, more cerebral cases, and leisure time to kick back after having photographed a cheating celebrity husband or two.

There was a black Jeep Wrangler parked off to the left of the outbuilding he'd passed on the driveway up to the main house, but there wasn't a soul in sight. Keane opened the door to his car and stepped out into the damp, humid air that contained the distinctive scent of ozone from the approaching lightning storm. It wouldn't be long before the rain hit and the fireworks began, but he still had enough time to make it through the wooden double doors.

Townes had mentioned this was an informal meeting, so Keane had dressed casual in a pair of khaki dress slacks and a light blue pullover, short-sleeved shirt he favored when golfing with the guys. He palmed the keys to the rental as he observed his surroundings, taking note of all the surveillance equipment as he continued walking.

Granted, the cameras were obscure enough to the untrained eye, but there was no likely avenue of approach to this property without being seen. Okay, so Calvert was a private man. Keane tried to shrug off the feeling that this job was anything other than what it had been presented to be.

"Keane, come on in before the storm hits," Townes called out, his deep voice barely carrying over the classical music drifting out of the Bose speakers overhead. The raspy tone made it sound as if Calvert had been punched in the throat one too many times.

Keane didn't have to shield his eyes from the sun since the cloud coverage had become thick with a storm veil. The Harley currently positioned near the entrance had quite a few missing parts, but that wasn't what caught him off guard. It was the appearance of Townes Calvert that gave him pause.

The man was wearing a pair of ripped jeans and an oil-stained dark blue T-shirt with a Bourbon Street Harley Davidson logo over the left pocket. His long hair was somewhat contained at the base of his neck, though a couple of long dark strands hung down the side of his left cheek—the same area where a two-inch scar traveled the length of his jawline and where the tattoo on his neck was now clearly visible.

There was a silver chain attached from Calvert's belt to what Keane assumed was the man's wallet. A vest hung off of a stool with multiple colorful badges, indicating he was a patched member to a 1% MC. He certainly looked the part at the moment, minus the classical music.

"Have any trouble finding the place?" Townes asked, wiping

his fingers off on a discolored rag before offering his hand. Keane didn't hesitate to return the handshake and flashed a smile.

"Not at all," Keane replied, liking this side of Calvert. This was a man who would invite his team over for a game on a Sunday afternoon, cook up a mean ribeye steak, and have a beer or two. He would have rubbed his hands together at the thought of his life finally coming together, but he refrained. "You ride. I used to own a softtail around six years ago, but life got in the way of allowing me time to enjoy it."

Keane took in the layout of the garage, impressed with the wooden cabinetry and matching shelves. Every imaginable tool and mechanic's equipment item was on hand for Calvert's use to do his own maintenance.

What was curious was the back of the large wooden structure. It appeared to be cordoned off with sheets of opaque plastic hanging from the ceiling and was currently under construction. The smell of the musty air had been replaced with grease and the unmistaken odor of copper wires being heated.

"This might be your chance to get that relatively small peace of mind back," Townes offered with what seemed to be a tone mixed with regret. He pointed over to a workbench before reaching for a small rolling chair. He compressed it with his weight, but the seat held up rather well under the man's solid frame. "Unfortunately, you might need to wait a month or two. Your first case came in faster than I'd anticipated."

Keane raised an eyebrow in question, wondering why he was being given the first case instead of the other four hires. Townes had shared with him that SSI would have a total of five men employed under his leadership. He'd oversee the investigations, but he wouldn't necessarily micromanage them if the guys maintained a handle on their business. He'd mentioned he was done being active in the field. He was merely a support role. Keane found that hard to believe.

"What shoe-shining wannabe drove up in that fuel-injected POS?"

Keane had picked up the file, surprisingly without a mark on it to blemish the cover, when a familiar voice called out from the back end of the building that had caught his attention earlier. There wasn't a chance in hell the man walking toward Keane wearing cargo shorts, a Hawaiian shirt, leather sandals, and sunglasses atop of his head was Brody Novak…but damned if it wasn't.

"One who has a limited budget," Keane countered with a smile, lifting an arm up and grasping Brody's hand. "How long has it been, man?"

"Too long," Brody replied, pulling away and pretending to look Keane over. "You sure as hell haven't changed. You realize that you'll have to get rid of those penny loafers if you want to live in the Sunshine State."

Keane laughed and shook his head, his fashion style having always been something the guys in his old unit gave him constant shit about. He had thick skin and dished out his fair share of horseshit to make it even. Brody had been with Keane on his last deployment to Afghanistan, in charge of the electronic communication systems the unit relied on.

"Sanderson is dressed just fine for his flight to D.C. later this afternoon," Townes reassured them as he continued to work on his V-Rod. He gestured toward the file in Keane's hand just as thunder rumbled above and the skies opened up outside the entrance. He didn't know those natural occurrences should have been perceived as an omen until he opened the file. "A friend of a friend is in need of some protection, leatherneck."

Keane stared at the black and white photograph of the one

woman who'd ever had the ability and opportunity to actually slice a relatively deep wound on his soul. He wanted to close the folder and go back to when Brody had recently joined them, maybe talk about old times or catch up with what they'd been doing for these last six years.

But this…this picture in front of him was the last thing he'd expected to set his eyes on after driving up such a tranquil private drive. It represented nothing but a thinly veiled illusion of the life he'd come to want but been denied.

"I know I'm probably not starting out on the right foot by saying this," Keane said after clearing his throat, "but I think Brody should take this one. Or one of the other three hires on your payroll."

"D.C.?" Brody inquired with interest. "I could—"

"I don't need to spell out the reason I chose you for this assignment." Townes continued working on his bike as if they were talking about what saddlebag would look better. Calvert sighed in resignation when Keane didn't respond and reached for the dirty rag he'd had earlier. He rolled back far enough to rest his right shoulder against the wooden shelf behind him. "Keane, Ashlyn Ellis has a rather important job that she can't just walk away from. I could send any one of the team members up there, but there's only one she'll truly trust to see that she's safe and you're well aware of that. I know there's some bad blood between the two of you, but she's seen up close and personal the lengths you'd go to in order to protect your charge."

"Ashlyn Ellis…as in the federal prosecutor who's in the papers concerning some threats that were made against her?" Brody whistled in disbelief and took a step back, as if saying he wanted nothing to do with their first assignment. Well, neither did Keane, but it didn't look as if he were being given a choice.

"I'd probably be better suited back here at headquarters researching some other bullshit."

"Headquarters?" Keane asked, grateful for something else to focus on instead of what was in his hand. He closed the file, not wanting to stare at Ashlyn's beautiful features any longer. He'd had that privilege in person and no longer needed a reminder of what could have been. "I thought we were going to be located somewhere in the city."

Calvert's land and residence was located in Sorrento, roughly thirty miles from downtown Orlando. Keane had already lined up a condo in the city and had been going to put down a deposit on the rental later this afternoon. It seemed as if that would have to take place later, although not if Keane was able to explain his plight.

"We're only here temporarily," Townes offered, still watching Keane's reactions through hooded eyes. "Brody has set up a network of servers in the back. I need him here. As for Coen, Royce, and Sawyer, they aren't due here for another week. That leaves you, buddy boy."

It didn't just *leave* Keane. The moment Calvert had taken this assignment, regardless that it was for a friend of a friend, he'd known of Keane and Ashlyn's previous relationship. Just how in-depth had his background check run? He didn't have anything to hide, but he certainly had his boundaries when it came to his private life.

"As for Federal Prosecutor Ashlyn Ellis," Calvert explained, regardless that Keane didn't want to hear it, "there hasn't been a specific threat to her life. Someone has been watching her very closely for the last few months and took things a little too far when the perp decided to enter her personal space. He or she was also monitoring the federal prosecutor in her own home through a breach in her security system, as well as her personal computer. Brody will be looking for this person's digital thumbprint, although that service is being provided complimentary. As I said, we aren't technically investigating this case. We're just providing Ashlyn Ellis with private security protection."

Calvert had said that last statement as if he thought Keane would want to dig deeper into the case he'd just been given, but that couldn't be further from the truth. He didn't want anything to do with it. He shared a look with Brody, who appeared at a loss as to what Keane's contention was with this assignment. He wouldn't know, considering his relationship with Ashlyn had occurred after his time with the Corps. Keane shook his head in warning, altering Brody that he really didn't want to know what was taking place.

The rain hadn't let up, and if anything, the elements outside the hulking maintenance bay had only gotten worse. Another round of lightning streaked across the sky, closely followed by a rumbling roll of thunder. Keane was envious of the storm's ability to let loose its rage. His was currently coiled inside of his chest, replacing the sense of freedom he'd had earlier.

"Is there anything else I need to know about SSI that you're currently keeping me in the dark about?" Keane asked, an edge to his tone that had Brody rocking back on the edge of his sandals. Every one of them at SSI had been hired for a reason. Calvert was well aware he was dealing with the best of the best, because he'd been the one to seek them out. Keane wouldn't apologize for being justifiably angry. "I'm beginning to think there ought to be a thirty-day probationary period to our contract."

Calvert threw his head back and barked out a laugh of what sounded like respect. He stood, grabbing a few of things that had been positioned on the shelf behind him and walked over to where Keane was standing, the two of them as different as night and day.

"You'll fit right in here, Sanderson." Townes was holding out a phone that didn't resemble any retail cellular device Keane had ever seen, along with a small black wallet and a bag. "Try to represent the firm in a professional manner and register your carry weapon with the local authorities upon your arrival in D.C. Call me if there's any trouble you can't handle."

CHAPTER THREE

"**G**OOD MORNING, SIMPSON," Ashlyn greeted as she walked past the security guard on duty outside the elevator access to the building from the underground garage. She'd already dropped her keys into her purse and had the straps over the shoulder of favorite black suit jacket. She was due in court within the hour and she refused to be late for pretrial discussion after what had taken place yesterday. "How are your studies coming along?"

"Finals are next month," Simpson replied, his usual infectious smile slightly fractured due to her circumstances. Ashlyn didn't like being the reason he was worried, but there wasn't anything she could say that would alleviate his concerns for her. Keeping that in mind, she did her best not to show that her left foot was still quite tender. The high heels she chose this morning didn't help, but the jurors took stock in professional appearances and she wouldn't look anything less than the well-practiced attorney she was. "Any trouble on the way in this morning?"

"No," Ashlyn answered gently with a shake of her head, refusing to look over her shoulder the way she had repeatedly when driving in to work this morning. It wasn't like her to have this constant fear inside that led to making decisions she otherwise would have considered out of character. It had to stop. She dropped her purse on the conveyer belt for Greta to scan. The older woman wasn't as friendly as Simpson was, but Ashlyn did get a nod of acknowledgement. "I'm sure Agent Coulter will have this wrapped up in no time."

Ashlyn slipped the thick leather strap of her father's old briefcase off her other shoulder as she put the rather large portfolio right behind her purse in its own tub. What she didn't put down was the disposable coffee cup in her right hand. She'd stopped at her usual place to get her daily cinnamon caramel latte. She wouldn't allow whoever was making her life hell to interfere with her already hectic pace. Changing her routine would only slow her down and her caseload wouldn't allow for that if she were to maintain her momentum on the court's calendar.

Agent Matthew Coulter had been assigned to her case and she'd given him all of her personal information, what little there was of it nowadays given the relentlessness of the caseload and the utter brutality of the suspects she'd been prosecuting. She'd even written down the names of those she'd faced in court, her neighbors that she never got a chance to talk to on a regular basis, the troop of doormen in her apartment building, the overtly opinionated barista who made her cinnamon caramel latte every morning, and even included the geeky pizza delivery boy who brought her a calzone two to three times a week. She didn't lead the most exciting life when you got down into the details, but the federal agent had assured her he would do what he could to find the individual who'd been stalking her these past few months.

"Agent Coulter was already here," Simpson revealed, motioning for Ashlyn to step forward underneath the metal detector. As usual, no alarms were sounded and she quickly started to gather up her items with her left hand. "Our shift had ended by the time he questioned the night shift late yesterday. He caught us bright and early at five o'clock this morning."

"See?" Ashlyn inquired with a positive attitude she didn't remotely feel. She caught sight of herself in the metal siding. Her professional appearance gave nothing away. "Agent Coulter is very good at his job. He hasn't been jaded by the system quite yet."

The entire federal building supporting the U.S. Attorney's office in D.C. now knew what had been transpiring for months. The FBI field office was just next door and the Director of Personnel for the DOJ had made a personal request on her behalf. The media was currently having a field day, and while that wasn't the approach she'd wanted to take, it was the way it played out because of the desires of the Public Affairs Office and the justice system—the same justice system she served as a federal prosecutor.

Ashlyn glanced once more at her blurred reflection in the metal side of the conveyer belt. There wasn't a strand out of place from the way she'd secured her light brown hair into a matching clip. Her crimson colored lipstick wasn't smeared as far as she could tell, despite the several sips of coffee she'd already taken. It was nice to see her efforts to look calm and collected this morning hadn't been wasted.

"Have a good day," Ashlyn called out before Simpson could ask her any more questions. She instantly felt the chill of the air-conditioned building sneak past the lining of her jacket. She'd made the right call to wear the matching black slacks instead of the skirt, seeing as it made her feel less vulnerable even with pantyhose on. Fortitude was what she needed at the moment…and a slice of bearing.

"Ashlyn, I heard what happened," Dennis Paavo said as he held open the elevator door for her as she approached. She smiled her appreciation and then hit both of their designated floors. A few more people from her department joined them, instantly crowding the small space. She managed to stay by the control panel since she was on the second floor. "Are you okay? Is there anything I can do?"

"Yes, and not right now. But thank you for offering, Dennis," Ashlyn reassured him, readjusting the straps on her shoulder while trying not to look uncomfortable. Dennis had asked her out for dinner a couple of times and she'd turned him down for various reasons. Bottom line was she just didn't have the time to have a personal life at this stage in her career. "The proper authorities are handling the case and I'm sure it won't be too long before it's resolved and the threat is taken care of soon."

"It'll be like trying to find a specific needle in a pile of needles," Adam said from his position in the back. He was one of the paralegals to Bishop Vance and had a penchant for office gossip and Goth clothing after hours. Ashlyn breathed a sigh of relief when the doors slid closed, hopefully shutting off anyone else's interest in further conversation. She'd known it would be like this, which was why she'd stayed home yesterday and met with the company representative for the security system installed in her apartment that had apparently been hacked. "Think about it. There are a number of people who could have it out for you. You've been successfully prosecuting cases for three years at a breakneck pace."

"As I said," Ashlyn managed to say without offending anyone the way she truly wanted to, "the proper authorities will look into it and deal with the perpetrator. We all know it's business as usual for any prosecutor. Oh, and Adam?"

Ashlyn breathed a sigh of relief when the elevator doors slid open and she was able to step right out, only turning to get one thought across before they closed.

"Please tell Bishop to stop. He's not poaching Mia from my team."

Ashlyn didn't miss the look of surprise that ran across Adam's face, or the smirk Dennis was currently sporting. Bishop Vance wasn't very well liked and neither was his team of vultures pecking at the edges of the more vulnerable team members. Their methods left a lot to be desired and most of the assistants kept their distance. Maybe having one of his pack of paralegal minions notify him that his backdoor dealings weren't quite so concealed as he'd imagined would give him pause. If not, she could always subtly mention his recent office ethics violation in their next department meeting and air his dirty laundry in public…not that anyone of the lead prosecutors still thought of him as any kind of angel.

"You have fifty-two minutes to be back downstairs," Gina announced as Ashlyn managed to finally make it to her destination. She gave a wave to her team of hard-charging go-getters, all four of them already at their desks buried within the maze of cubicles swilling coffee. She acknowledged them before walking into her office to set her stuff down next to her desk. "Chief Garner wants to meet with you beforehand, Victor Wright is sending over an IT technician to review your desktop computer, Mia and Parker are currently up on the schedule to go with you to court today, and Mr. Rutledge would like to confer with you on the Haung case before he schedules depositions for next week."

"Chief Garner will have to wait until I'm back from court this afternoon. I need to confer with my witness one more time before he goes on the stand today, which means I'm leaving here in the next five minutes for conference room 5B downstairs." Ashlyn set down her coffee and then rummaged through her purse for her phone. She could already see the list of missed messages, but she had a time constraint this morning. She switched her cell phone to silent before sliding it into the back pocket of the leather portfolio. It wouldn't do to have it ring during court. The very sight of a cellular device inside a federal courtroom could send some judges into the stratosphere. She'd even heard that Judge Randolph had crushed Bishop's iPhone with his gavel in open court. "Call Victor and tell him I'd like to see him around five o'clock today. I want Parker to stay in my office with the technician, especially since Agent Coulter is having his own specialist confirm that nothing has been disturbed on my work computers. Parker has the most computer knowledge on the team and I don't want anything botched at this point. If even one of my working files goes missing, I'll have Victor's entire department crucified. Oh, and try to schedule Rutledge in tomorrow before lunch."

Ashlyn had spent the time looking at the other message slips on her desk in reference to incoming phone traffic, deeming them relatively unimportant…at least for the timeframe of her pending appearance. There wasn't anything of urgency that couldn't wait until the end of the week, maybe even late tomorrow. She picked up her briefcase and her coffee before heading for the door. She barely managed not to appear irritated at the man who currently stood at the threshold.

Jarod Garner was the Chief of the Criminal Division that oversaw her department, as well as many others, and he was in fact very good at his job of supervising the administration of the division. That didn't mean she could just drop whatever she was doing to speak with him regarding the very topic he'd dismissed out of hand three months ago.

Unfortunately, those in Ashlyn's line of work had their fair share of threats and intimidations from those on the opposite

side of the law. She was lucky to get through any given week
without some corrupt criminal defendant threatening to kill her
in some depraved way.

The majority of emails, letters, and various packages sent to
the U.S. Attorney's Building in D.C. addressed to federal
prosecutors were vetted through a jointly operated U.S.
Government/Postal Service facility which specialized in
detecting all manner of threats. Ninety-nine percent of the
mail—including all kinds of packages—were discerned to be
nonthreatening and distributed through a secure service to the
mailroom in the basement of the building.

It was only when some letter or parcel was detected and
proved to be a risk through a battery of determining methods
that the item was rendered hazardous and the FBI was called in
to take a closer look. The FBI always took lead because
delivering a threat, either materially or by unlawful communication, through the U.S. Postal Service was a federal crime and one
her office would prosecute once the FBI made the case.

"I don't have time right now, sir," Ashlyn said, managing to
look pointedly at her silver watch without spilling her latte. "I'm
due in court. I told Gina to contact your office. I should be back
around five o'clock."

"We need to talk," Jarod advised in a concerned tone that
made Ashlyn even more on edge than she already was. His usual
air of confidence seemed slightly rattled, but he gave nothing
away. His navy blue suit didn't have a bit of lint on the fabric
and there wasn't a strand out of place of his black hair that was
peppered with grey. It was something in his mannerisms that
told her he was tense. "Five o'clock. No later. And you don't
leave for any reason beforehand."

Ashlyn almost called Jarod back into her office, but then
decided against it. Had there been an immediate threat of life

and death, he wouldn't be waiting until later this afternoon to talk to her. She started toward the door before being held up once more.

"Morning, Ms. Ellis," Paul acknowledged, a small black bag of tools in his hand. He was one of the better IT technicians who came calling whenever there was an issue with the network and tended to stay too long at Gina's desk. "Victor sent me down to take a look at your computer. He wants—"

"It's okay, Paul," Ashlyn answered, trying not to sound too abrupt. She figured she had less than fifty minutes now, where she would then be en route for the Federal Courts via the secure shuttle service. She still needed time to address her team and meet with her witness. "Please give Parker the report on whatever you find, so that he can forward it on to Special Agent Coulter."

"Of course," Paul replied as he stepped aside to let her pass by. Gina stayed behind to talk to him, giving Ashlyn the distraction she needed to finally escape the magnetic pull of her office. "I need…"

Ashlyn finally made it to the front entrance of the cubicles. Her team consisted of four paralegals; all of whom she'd handpicked herself. The talent standing before her—Mia Hernandez, Parker Davis, Aiden Younger, and Reed Foster— was astounding. Now she had to give them an update and also a briefing on what today held for them.

"Parker, I hate to do this to you again," Ashlyn said honestly, but having no other choice but to leave him behind. "I need you to stay here."

Ashlyn took five minutes she didn't have and gave additional details of what had transpired over the course of yesterday. Gina would keep them apprised, but Parker needed to understand why she requested he stay behind. It wasn't long before Mia and

Aiden fell into step with her as they proceeded to the lobby. Reed stayed behind to plow through some preceding case law that had similar attributes and might provide some precedence that might be able to help during closing arguments, if not provide her with a motion for the case to force the court's hand.

"Do you need to switch shoes?" Mia asked once they were inside the elevator.

"Is it that obvious?" Ashlyn asked, raising an eyebrow in question. She leaned back against the laminate wood to catch her breath. This was the chaotic atmosphere she usually thrived in and all she could think of was that she would love to be back in her office with the door shut to keep away everything and everyone. She didn't have that luxury, just as she couldn't afford for anyone to see a weakness. She exhaled and then straightened away from the wall right before the doors slid open. "I appreciate the offer, but I'm fine. Let's get this day started."

HOW COULD SHE act as if she hadn't betrayed him?

He'd even reached out to her, brushing his hand against hers…so warm and inviting. He hadn't meant to close his eyes and he was relieved to see no one had noticed anything other than an innocent gesture. Her response had left little to be savored. She hadn't even noticed his touch. It was like some vile enemy had turned her against him.

Red-hot coals were being raked against his heart and she couldn't even see his pain due to her dependence on this circus of distractions. She was turning out like the others when he'd thought she was different.

He drummed his fingers on the desk and listened to the calming rhythm, but all the incessant noise did was stir the anger that clung to him like the sweet fragrance of her perfume.

He couldn't wait any longer for her to come to him.

It was time.

CHAPTER FOUR

KEANE SURVEYED THE United States Attorney Office's building from his position across 4th Street NW, in the parking lot of the Juvenile Probation Office on the eastern side of Judiciary Square. He held the coffee he'd gotten at Jack's Famous Deli down the street as he studied the layout for which someone could monitor the comings and goings of the employees. There were multiple points of entry, although that would most likely not concern the perpetrator the feds were currently looking for. Whoever was targeting Ashlyn Ellis was already well aware of her routine and had watched at great length for several months.

The cool weather brought by the dipping sun and endless rows of icy concrete facades bereft of any warmth had put a nip in the air, but the chill he felt in his bones could very well be from his last memory of Ashlyn. Keane pushed the visual away as he gazed up at the multiple levels of blackened windows. He recalled from the dossier he'd gone over on the plane that Ashlyn's office was located on the second floor. Unless their suspect had specialized optics equipment to penetrate the tint, a vantage point located outside of her office wasn't the place from which she could be observed.

Keane answered his cell phone when it chimed without

looking at the display. He'd already called his sister and dad to let both of them know he'd be out of touch for a while on a case. That left some old friends back in California south of L.A. or his current employer. He was betting on the latter.

"Sanderson."

"Calvert wants twelve hour check-ins—either voice or electronic. The details are in the email he sent you covering your case," Brody announced, giving Keane the victory. It was rather hollow seeing as he was the only one celebrating his small feat. "Coen should be arriving in Florida tomorrow morning and I hear he's got some connections up in D.C. that you might be able to use, because I have nothing so far on this surveillance feed that was hijacked."

"How is that possible?" Keane questioned while at the same time wondering what kind of contacts Coen Flynn could possibly have that Calvert didn't. "I was never into all that tech shit, but isn't there some way to locate an IP address for this asshole?"

"And now I know why you were in the field while I was back at basecamp making sure your ass was clear of fire and headed in the right fucking direction," Brody muttered, not bothering to cover up his words too much. His irritability did cause Keane to smile at the memories of their last deployment together. It was nice to have someone have his six that he already had an established friendship with. "Listen, it's simple. Whoever you're dealing with is good at the technical aspect and knows how to cover his tracks. Calvert doesn't want to step on anyone's toes without good reason fresh out of the gate, so we're still only under contract for offering protection services."

Keane understood what Brody was conveying and actually agreed with the assessment to keep a low profile. Safeguard Security & Investigations was just getting off of the ground.

Calvert had them licensed as a private and government contracting firm, meaning their clearances allowed them cases that needed to be handled with a little discretion. This assignment had only been contracted for protection…nothing else. He would do well to remember that and provide said services while staying out of the FBI's investigation.

"I'm about to meet with the special agent in charge. I'll let you know if he can find his ass with either hand," Kean revealed, leaning up against Matthew Coulter's building. He removed his shades and slipped the glasses into the inner pocket of his suit jacket. The sun had now set behind the building. It wouldn't be long before the streetlights flickered to life on this side of the hill, along with the D.C. nightlife making another grand appearance. The movers and shakers would be heading to dinner and their chosen forms of entertainment soon. D.C. would take on the manifestation of the new world Sodom once again. He wanted to be long gone from here by then. The monsters who inhabited those shadows were best left on their own. "I'll exchange information with him and create a rapport. Better to be on his good side than appear to be hindering his efforts."

A man walked out of the building's main exit to Keane's left, but it wasn't Agent Coulter. Calvert had the man's file included in Ashlyn's case file. He stood at five feet and ten inches with short blond hair and blue eyes. He had a solid but limited reputation and also had a decent percentage when it came to closing difficult cases. Ashlyn was in good hands all the way around, even if she didn't quite know it yet. Keane would still like to follow up that written assessment in person.

"Calvert is most likely to send Coen up there if you need backup," Brody offered, sounding somewhat distracted as he pecked at his keyboards. Keane could hear what sounded like beeping and could picture his friend in front of a bank of computer monitors. "I'll be your eyes and ears if needed. We have access to the local CCTV feeds. By the way, how's that coffee tasting?"

"You can see me right now, can't you?" Keane asked, lowering the brown cup he'd been about to take a drink from. He narrowed his gaze to take in the various streetlights and poles before focusing on the building across the street in front of them. "Did you just hack into the surveillance feeds of the U.S. Government municipal buildings or did we get permission?"

"It's good to work with you again too, Sanderson," Brody said with a laugh. "We'll have to get caught up over beers when you're back in the Sunshine State where the weather is considerably warmer. By the way, I went ahead and ordered some shirts for you. We can't have you sticking out like a sore thumb."

"What about Royce and Sawyer?" Keane asked, curious as to when the other two team members were due to arrive. It would have been more beneficial to meet them before being given an assignment. "I thought Calvert said they were arriving in Orlando by the week's end."

"That's the plan for now. I'm not sure how much interaction each of you will have on one another's cases," Brody responded with reservation. Keane's attention was pulled off the building in front of him when Matthew Coulter stepped out of the glass doors to Keane's left. He tossed what was left of his coffee in the metal trashcan and stepped forward. "There's your man now. Keep me posted."

Keane shot an annoyed look across the street, knowing full well Brody had caught the slight. They already had one individual doing illicit surveillance of a government official. They didn't need an issue of that sort with this case.

"Agent Coulter?" Keane called out to grab the other man's attention. He extended his hand with his credentials displayed in his left. "Keane Sanderson. SSI."

"I'm glad you called earlier," Coulter said as he returned the gesture with a slightly distracted look around them. He then indicated they should walk next door to the U.S. Attorney's Office Building. "This case isn't going to be as straightforward as I initially thought it was going to be. It's a good thing Chief Garner requested outside personal protection in the meantime."

"What do you mean it's not going to be straightforward?" Keane asked, waiting for the traffic indicator to signify they could use the crosswalk on F Street NW safely. He was used to the wall-to-wall traffic during the commuting hours, especially living in Los Angeles, but that didn't mean he'd ever grown used to wasting his life in the churning mass of humanity. "This guy must have left some kind of footprint. You're telling me your cyber analysis group couldn't find anything on this perp?"

"That's exactly what I'm telling you. This guy has talent and used Ms. Ellis' lack of knowledge of cyber vulnerability to his advantage." Agent Coulter stepped off the corner and proceeded to walk in the pedestrian zone. The lighted displays appeared brighter now that the sun was setting. Keane had no choice but to follow when all he really wanted was a place to discuss this in private. "I'd like access to Ms. Ellis' apartment, preferably tonight. We need to do a full sweep for any devices that may have been hidden on the premises without her knowledge."

That would explain why Coulter's intention was to enter the U.S. Attorney Office's building. All Keane had wanted was to obtain more information on the investigation before meeting with Ashlyn. It was bound to be uncomfortable at first and he didn't think she'd want an audience. He sure as hell didn't, but it appeared that's what he was going to get.

"I'm sure that won't be a problem. She's shown her desire to cooperate thus far," Keane replied as he ran the facts over through his mind while coming to a conclusion. He needed time to look over the layout of Ashlyn's office and meet her staff, as well as anyone else she came in contact with on a daily basis. "What about her office and the technology she uses there? Computer? Phone?"

"One of our agents stopped by Ms. Ellis' office this morning with one of their best guys and they found jack," Coulter revealed as he walked up to the double glass entrance of Ashlyn's building. He stopped just short of pulling the door open and was clearly puzzled by what he was about to say. "Her office computer and desk phone were clear, as far as we can tell with the best IT folks we have. It does sort of make me wonder if this individual feels he doesn't need to monitor her at work or doesn't have to use her system to do the surveillance. He sure as hell appears to have the capability without anyone being the wiser."

Keane comprehended what Coulter was saying and his assumptions weren't going to make a lot of people very happy with the implications. No one would envy the position this just put him in and Calvert no doubt knew how this would eventually play out if it was an inside job. Background checks were about to be rerun on every individual working inside the federal prosecutor's office building in D.C., which would undoubtedly make some employees rather uncomfortable. It might even run amuck of the union officials representing the federal office workers. That had shitstorm written in bold letters all over it.

"I'll establish a varied schedule so that Ashlyn isn't in the same place at predictable times. Maybe we can define some of our potential suspect pool by process of elimination," Keane proposed, reaching into his jacket for his credentials and presenting himself at the security checkpoint as he bypassed the metal detector. "Give me one minute."

Keane broke away from Coulter to speak with one of the security guards on duty, alerting him to the fact that Chief Garner had left specific instructions to permit Keane through with his weapon as he checked in with his proof of clearance, official visit request, U.S. Government contractor's license number, and a concealed carry permit issued for federal law enforcement contractors. It wasn't long before he'd stepped around the metal detector, had his status verified, and had his weapon logged as permitted past security.

"You speak of Ms. Ellis as if you know her," Agent Coulter pointed out, having followed the same routine with the exception of only showing his FBI identification and badge to the guards and being allowed through without further delay. He pointed to the elevator bank straight ahead. "Isn't your firm based out of Florida?"

Keane could have said he'd yet to spend the night in the Sunshine State, but didn't want to get into specifics now that strangers surrounded them in their bid for the elevator. Someone had already pressed the button and all they could do now was wait. He kept his answer brief.

"We've met previously."

A lone ding resounded through the lobby followed by the swoosh of the elevator doors opening. It was the end of the day and there were more people exiting than there were entering. It took a moment for the transfer of humanity, but eventually the small group of people standing alongside Keane and Coulter were finally ascending to their ultimate destination.

The short ride was made in silence as they disembarked on the second floor, although Keane did take time to memorize the faces of those beside him. He'd watched their movements in their reflections on the polished plastic of the employee information board. He'd always had the ability to recall the smallest of details while quickly learning the habits of others. The man standing directly in front of Keane lowered his right shoulder every six seconds, most likely due to an old sports injury. He didn't have the bearing normally associated with former military members. The woman looking up at the display numbers blinked rapidly in unease every time the gentleman behind her cleared his throat, which had only been twice in the man's defense. She was either a germaphobe or she'd been abused in some way to cause such a strong reaction. Either way, the blonde showed a dislike for him and his proximity to her.

"An established rapport should make your job that much easier," Coulter said after they'd vacated the elevator and started down the hallway. Keane purposefully slowed his steps so he could evaluate his surroundings. "Although Ms. Ellis wasn't too accepting of my suggestion that she vary her routine. You'll have your work cut out for you, since she's so determined to act as if this isn't a major problem for her."

Keane was well aware of just how dedicated Ashlyn was to her profession. Neither one of them had been willing to give up their careers and established lives for one another. Could they have handled ending their relationship on better terms, given their respective situations? Absolutely, but they hadn't. It had ended badly. Cruel words had been exchanged and the only way past that was through time, regret, and forgiveness. He chalked it up to both of them being passionate beings who laid their hearts on the line, only to fail at the most intimate of times. Would she be able to let bygones be bygones?

"Agent Coulter, may I help you?"

The woman who'd called out to Coulter was rather petite with short auburn hair and black-rimmed glasses. It was as if she was trying to present a professional appearance and yet maintain the air of a sexy librarian for those willing to pay attention to her quirks. She was standing behind her desk, where her nameplate was visible. Keane didn't have to read it to know this was Gina Nelson, Ashlyn's administrative assistant and seasoned right hand. Her photograph, along with her biography, had been included in the files Calvert had supplied to Keane. The bit about her annual trips to Acapulco with her college sorority sisters had been interesting enough to warrant a second read through.

"Yes, I need to speak with Ms. Ellis regarding her case."

Gina had given Keane a cursory glance, but apparently concluded he was some kind of federal agent as well, not missing the mark by very much. He didn't bother to correct her assumption. Conjectures could be very helpful in his business of working on limited information and extracting the truth from those who didn't wish to give it. He'd rather not have to explain who he was just yet, and quite honestly, why burst her bubble of self-assured indulgence?

Keane, to be quite honest, wasn't so sure Ashlyn would actually see him if Gina revealed his identity.

CHAPTER FIVE

"**H**OW COULD YOU possibly believe that I would go along with this?" Ashlyn asked, shrugging off her suit jacket in what came down to annoyance rather than rage. She defaulted to simple irritation because she still believed in her heart of hearts that this blunder could be rectified. She didn't like when other people made decisions for her, thinking they were acting in her best interest, and she certainly didn't appreciate it when the results affected her personal life. She'd uncharacteristically asked for two favors out of an abundance of interoffice diplomacy. Both of them were well-deserved, but Jarod Garner did not have the right to bring in an outside firm when her case had already been assigned to the FBI as per protocol. It hadn't been his place to do so without discussing the appearance of impropriety with her and she wasn't going to stand still for his lording over her. "You should have consulted with me, first and foremost."

"It's a necessary measure and you know that to be true. This now has national media coverage and we have no concept of how this individual is going to react to what appears to be your rejection of him."

Rejection? Ashlyn shook her head at Jarod's insinuation that she'd somehow been the one to seek out the unwanted attention she'd been receiving from this individual. She was forced to remind herself that this wasn't Jarod's doing and that he was only trying to help resolve a difficult situation.

"Call Mr. Calvert back and inform him we won't be needing his services in the foreseeable future," Ashlyn instructed, scanning her desk as she walked past it to the small closet in the corner. She pulled out a hanger and slid the ends of the red cherry wood and chromed steel construction through the sleeves of her jacket. "These Machiavellian machinations that have been perpetrated upon myself through no fault of my own are officially in the hands of the FBI and I want this investigation to stay that way. I'm sure Special Agent Coulter wouldn't appreciate the interference of an up-gunned personal security firm."

Ashlyn had been out of her office for most of the morning and afternoon dealing with spurious defense motions and a senior citizen hard-nosed Jackie Onassis wannabe court clerk with illusions of grandeur. Gina had held down the fort, but there were several messages in the middle of her desk marked urgent that were currently waiting for her immediate response. They would have to wait a little longer until she'd taken some ibuprofen for the headache she'd been fighting all day. She silently closed the closet door, wishing she could just as easily shut away all of her fears and frustrations. It was just like the surf on the beach—relentlessly pounding the shores of her perception.

Per her instructions this morning, Parker had sent detailed text messages throughout the day updating her on what the IT technician had discovered while combing through the log files on her desktop computer. Apparently, Paul had installed additional vertical and horizontal firewalls for her protection under the orders of his department's supervisor and an Agent Freeman with the FBI's Cyber Crimes Division, who had verified that her work system had not been tampered with in any manner. That was all good news, as far as Ashlyn was concerned.

Most of the files she worked with were archived here on her desktop and on the department's main server. If any of her work product had been compromised, it would have caused her to file advisory notifications with the courts in all of the cases that data was suspected to have been affected. Judges were like old women when it came to losing control of the chain of evidence concerning their cases. It was a violation of their dominion and someone was going to pay the price. Of course, that would result in the courts' bias turning against the U.S. Attorney's Office and her as their advocate.

With that said…it had still been one hell of a day for justice.

"In my department's defense, the attention this creature had been previously paying to you three months ago wasn't nearly as threatening as these most recent escalations," Jarod replied cautiously as he took a seat in one of the guest chairs after unloading a stack of bundled files onto the floor. The other chair was hopelessly buried and would take a shovel to clear. Ashlyn understood Jarod didn't want her to press the issue of the lateness to which her plight was now garnering attention. "We went by clearly established protocol."

"For Christ's sake, Jarod, are you already trying to mitigate the responsibility for your lack of response to my earlier warnings about this guy? Just shoot me now! Protocol didn't stop this man from finding out where I lived and then watching my every move in my own home," Ashlyn pointed out, practically forcing those words through her clenched teeth. She refused to be a victim like every damned defendant she interviewed. Nothing was ever their fault. According to them, everything would have been just perfect in their little slice of the world if the government had just left them alone. It was truly a damn shame it had taken this long to investigate the unwanted attention she'd been given early on. "For all I know, this pervert is sitting on my toilet watching me shower every morning and searching through my trash after I leave for work to garner hints on what to buy me for my birthday. A federal agent and our own IT people stopped by my office this morning and went through my computer. It appears the only place I'm being watched is in my own home and outside of these glass and metal walls. Which reminds me, I gave Agent Coulter access to all the emails I forwarded to your team to investigate. The most recent letters, too. Oh, and of course the small gifts sent to me over the last few months. I told him I had already given the items in question to your people, but he still wants them for evidence. I'm hoping this can be wrapped up quickly, because the Glasson case is coming to a close. Closing arguments should take place by the end of the week, and I don't want to have to go through an evidentiary hearing with Judge Gilroy over the chain of custody of our forensic accounting files and the fourteen months of investigations and depositions of our expert witnesses."

"I requested that Victor take a look at your private security system and discuss any vulnerabilities with their technical support staff." Jarod's cell phone vibrated in his suit jacket, but he ignored it after a casual glance. As usual, he pointed out his awareness that she planned a long night in the office. Ashlyn didn't react to his witless statement, for he understood the nature of this business and he certainly recognized why she would rather be here safe at work. She logged in long, hard hours and most of the resources she needed to complete that task were here in this building. "He'll need access to your apartment and he'll most likely want to walk you through whatever changes that will be implemented."

"I'll see if Victor can arrange to be there first thing in the morning. Otherwise, he'll have to schedule an appointment for the suspect to let him in and go over the changes with him," Ashlyn replied with a tight smile, not willing to surrender the hours needed to prepare, construct, and rehearse her closing arguments. Okay, maybe she was being too harsh about this situation, but she'd had enough. She was tired, stressed, and the fear was starting to take hold. It wasn't something she was comfortable with. At least Mia and Aiden were staying to go over today's testimony from the defense's expert witness. It was going to be a long night and she made a mental note to have Gina order Chinese food for three before she left for the day. "I'll give him call in a few minutes once the roar in my head settles out."

Jarod continued to disregard the person trying to reach him. There wasn't a minute of the day that the man wasn't being beckoned by someone for some emergency or another. Ashlyn appreciated his steadfast attention now, knowing full well he was most likely needed elsewhere, but she could have used it three months ago when this thing could have been squashed in its infancy.

Ashlyn pulled out her desk chair, grateful the dark brown leather was comfortable as she sank down into its embracing depths. She took one moment to herself, inhaling deeply to try and ease her rushing headache. It didn't work.

"You know how this works, Ashlyn," Jarod said with a slight hint of a reprimand. Ashlyn raised an eyebrow, not willing to allow him that luxury. He wasn't technically her direct supervisor. He only had administrative overview of her department. She worked for the Department of Justice and for the Attorney General in all the ways that mattered. He certainly didn't get to berate her on how she conducted her business. Victor Wright ran the cyber division and happened to be a good friend of Ashlyn's. She didn't need Jarod telling her where those boundaries lay or who she trusted with her personal security. "We're stretched thin. The Chenglei Haung case is only the half of it. The Chinese government is behind ninety percent of what they're fronting as a privately owned company."

Ashlyn understood just how important the Haung case was to the DOJ and the current administration. The defendant had been involved in the illegal export of classified material, specifically dual use technology that was a restricted export item controlled and plainly identified under International Traffic in Arms Regulations (ITAR) agreements. The company had clearly falsified the end user certificate. It was a serious offense and the lead prosecutor on the case, Andrew Rutledge, was having a tough time proving Haung Enterprises was the one responsible and not the U.S. Defense Contractor that held the proprietary rights to the technology. She didn't overlook that Rutledge had wanted to consult on the case either and assumed Gina had taken care of scheduling a meeting for tomorrow to go over the contractor's depositions that were going to be key in the prosecution of the case.

"I'm well aware of how busy Victor is," Ashlyn countered, reaching into her draw for the bottle of Motrin she always kept on hand. She first squeezed then unscrewed the cap and shook out two of the orange capsules. "He can send someone else over in the morning then. He doesn't have to handle it personally. He has good people."

Ashlyn stood and walked across the carpeted floor, wishing she could have kicked off her heels. She would never appear anything other than professional in front of Jarod though, so she toughed out the soreness that still remained from where the shard of glass had embedded itself on that horrible night. She poured herself some water from the pitcher she kept on the small side table beside the coffee maker. She tossed the two pills into her mouth and then washed them down before walking back to her desk, cataloging what was to be left of her evening.

"Fine. Call Victor and set something up for tomorrow morning, but don't wait too long. Give him time to assign one of his people before the end of the day. As for Safeguard Security & Investigations, they're a good alternative for personal security while the FBI investigates the case." Jarod appeared firm in his stance on contracting out her protection away from the office. Ashlyn could hear his cell phone rattle once more and wondered if he ever got tired of being at the end of that leash. "You and I both know it's most likely some momma's boy who has a thing for women in power because his mother never cut the apron strings. Maybe he saw you in court or he sweeps up the grass clippings around your apartment complex. Either way, he's taken things a step too far and will most likely run for the hills the moment he realizes the feds are nipping at his heels."

"A step too far?" Ashlyn repeated in complete disgust, leaning back in her chair and wishing she could take the tight clip out of her hair. The throbbing in her temples had only gotten worse as the child pornography case currently on her docket came to a close. If only they could send these scumbags away forever and never have to worry about them seeing the light of day again. Add in the stress of not knowing how far this fanatic was willing to take things had her one step away from snapping Jarod's head clean off. "Are you paying attention at all? Let me explain to you in detail why we aren't just dealing with some random lawn care guy who's *taken things a step too far.* Sending me complimentary emails on my looks and clothing were nonthreatening. Sending me small gifts in the mail to my office were nonthreatening. The moment this guy started leaving notes on my vehicle saying he'd find a way for us to be together changed the tone of what we're dealing with. He's delusional and believes we have a relationship.

He's only escalated from there and now he knows where I live, *watching* me in the privacy of my own home. That wasn't a step too far, Jarod. What this guy did was commit a felony and it isn't a sporting event where he can be forgiven for committing a foul."

"Which is why I called Townes Calvert," Jarod replied, confident in his decision to recruit outside assistance. He rested an ankle over his leg as he settled in to explain his reasoning. His confidence didn't bolster hers in the least. "He's an old friend from my military days who recently went into business for himself. As I said earlier, the firm's name is Safeguard Security & Investigations. SSI is now one of our new first-line contractors. Every hire Calvert employs has a military background with experience on a high-priority protective detail, a solid reputation, and a security clearance the government will maintain during their time working for SSI. The company will provide you protection until Agent Coulter can resolve this problem of ours. Calvert is sending someone to watch over you twenty-four seven until this is resolved. His gentleman should be here within the hour."

"There's no way in hell I'm allowing someone to shadow my every move, Jarod," Ashlyn warned off, looking past him to see Victor Wright standing in her doorway. She waved him in, grateful for the interruption and a chance to make Jarod see that she didn't need round-the-clock security when all of this was going to be over in the next day or so. "This child pornography case is closed from any media coverage and I won't take the chance of any information being leaked until a verdict is handed down. Victor, tell Jarod you'll make it so that my apartment is more secure than Fort Knox. You'll make it impossible for this guy to have the capability to watch me in the privacy of my own home."

"You're assuming we're looking for a man. And I wish it were that simple," Victor said somewhat regretfully with a slow shake of his head. Ashlyn's headache was now on the verge of a full-blown migraine. "Whoever hacked into your security feeds and private network is damned good at covering his or her tracks. I know this has been handed off to the FBI, but I had a few spare minutes today. This perp has no traceable digital footprint that we can track down to any one specific person or any money trail leading to a bank account with any kind of significant amount of funds. Finding this type of person isn't going to be easy."

"What exactly are you saying?" Ashlyn asked cautiously, refusing to believe that such an evidence trail couldn't be followed. Even Chenglei Haung, backed by the full resources of a major world power, had left a digital footprint for Victor's team to follow. "Are you saying the individual we're looking for is some type of professional?"

"I'm saying that since Jarod wanted me to upgrade your security system, I took the time to look at how this individual was able to access the network. He or she is better than most of the experts I employ here in our IT department, Ashlyn. I mean, we're talking this person might even be considerably better than anyone on my team."

Victor looked at the buried guest chair next to Jarod, spreading his hands open in a gesture of defeat and decided to lean against the wall. He'd always been proud of his abilities and there had never been a case given to him where he wasn't able to prove innocence or guilt. Now he was standing here telling her the man or woman who'd become fixated on her couldn't be rooted out of the system.

"Look, this is going to have to be investigated from the ground up by Agent Coulter and their cyber terrorist unit.

Effective network monitoring needs to be done in order to find active efforts to bypass your security measures. Coulter came into my office asking if we'd seen anything unusual on our networks. We haven't, but I did share with him what I found on your private network. He no doubt already has his cyber super geeks department all over it, but I'll keep following the endless trail of digital footprints this hacker has used to disguise his efforts," Victor promised, lifting one side of his mouth in what was most likely supposed to be a reassuring smile. He failed...miserably. Ashlyn hadn't considered this wouldn't be an easy thing to resolve. How could this guy circumvent the entire technology and information systems' security efforts of the United States government? "Ashlyn, I'll follow you home when you're ready. I have one of our technicians coming with me and he'll install a new firewall system that far surpasses your old one."

Ashlyn's desk phone emitted a low-toned beep, indicating it was an internal call. She glanced at the black and silver unit and confirmed it was Gina. Work didn't cease for personal issues, but she had been hoping for a moment's reprieve to gather her thoughts.

"Yes, Gina?" Ashlyn inquired after leaning forward and pressing the speaker button, doing her best to keep the despair out of her tone.

"Agent Coulter is here to see you," Gina announced, her professional manner telling Ashlyn the man was standing next to her assistant's desk instead of taking a seat in the small row of chairs opposite her door. "Along with another agent."

Ashlyn was a bit surprised by Agent Coulter's visit. Was he here to tell her he'd figured out who had been stalking her? It was the only way to realistically view what had been happening to her over the last few months. The implied intimacy of the emails had left her feeling somewhat uneasy, but the letters and gifts had caused her to be downright worried for her safety and that of her team. She'd taken self-defense classes and was very proficient at shooting a weapon, but that didn't mean she wanted to test any of those skillsets.

It wasn't as if Ashlyn had time to have a personal life. Yes, she would spend an occasional evening with a man who understood her free-time limitations, given her profession. She had needs and she saw to them when time permitted. For the most part, she'd spent the majority of every waking hour since she'd graduated law school advancing her career to its current level. Now was no time to rest on her laurels and she'd like to continue marching forward without the threat of some jerk popping up in her apartment one evening hanging over her head.

"Send them in, please," Ashlyn finally instructed in resignation, knowing full well her team of paralegals were most likely wondering why the chief of the criminal division, the head of their cyber unit, and now two federal agents were gathering in her tiny office. She'd have to meet with them soon to give them an update on the situation and she was hoping to announce an arrest had been made. "Let's hope he…"

Ashlyn's words trailed off as Gina appeared in the doorway with only one federal agent and someone else entirely. Both Jarod and Victor turned around at the sight of the obvious surprise written across her face, no doubt wondering what had brought about the utter destruction of the most enduring poker face they'd been acquainted with. The other man…well, he wasn't with the FBI. He was from her past. He was also her one and only regret.

"Ashlyn, it's good to see you again. I'm sorry it's under these circumstances."

Ashlyn could feel the intensity of Jarod's curious gaze, but she didn't know how to show any other emotion than dumbfounded surprise as she slowly stood from her desk chair. It didn't matter that she broke out in a light perspiration or the fact that her heart was experiencing a slight twinge of pain. She'd learned long ago to never display what she was thinking in the courtroom. She had that practiced air about her and it had never failed her before today. It put her at a disadvantage and that was the last thing she needed right now.

Jarod stood and Victor pushed off the wall as they turned to make introductions to the man who would be protecting her twenty-four seven. Gina had it wrong. The man standing next to her wasn't a federal agent nor did he work with Agent Coulter. That left only one reason he would be here and Ashlyn couldn't wrap her mind around that with any amount of clarity. This couldn't be happening. Not now. It was the perfect storm and she wasn't ready for the explosive impact.

SSI would just have to send another one of their agents to do the job. Her heart wasn't capable of beating this hard for that long. This man was already biased toward her welfare and it was through no fault of her own. He would have to go for the good of all concerned.

Keane Sanderson.

The man who had singlehandedly saved an entire courtroom of innocent people from the threat of death.

The man who Ashlyn rejected when he'd asked for more than she could give and vanished before she could realize her own mistake.

He hadn't changed in the five years since she'd seen him last. His dark brown hair was still cut short, but not short enough to prevent the soft waves from lying in the exact manner in which he'd trained it this morning. His matching brown eyes were flecked with gold and she recalled that those specks lit up when he was content. She realized he wasn't remotely pleased at the moment either and the muscle along his jawline was as taut as a guitar string with what she assumed was irritation.

"Keane," Ashlyn managed to say without the tremor she knew to be at the back of her throat. She forced her legs to move and walk around her desk. She made the mistake of breathing in when he was close enough to shake hands. He wore the same captivating cologne he wore all those years ago, and she had to mentally block the memories of their time together as she steeled herself for the heat of his hand. She failed miserably. "It's been quite a long time."

ALL HE'D WANTED to do was love her.

Why couldn't she have just returned his affection like she wanted to?

He drummed his fingers on the fabric of his pants, wishing he could hear the soothing, rhythmic sounds of her sleeping breath to ease the rage building inside of his head.

Now things had to change. She needed to accept God's truth.

CHAPTER SIX

KEANE HAD PURPOSEFULLY chosen to survey the small office before focusing on Ashlyn Ellis. The elegant décor was all her. She liked the polished appearance that stated professionalism. That was evident through the vintage hand-tooled oak furniture, as well as the small collection of leather-bound classic books with gilded edges that revolved around justice system and the Constitution. The warmth of the earth tones was meant to put people at ease and yet there was a formal air to the room, almost as if the office was meant to prevent a person from seeing behind the pretense.

His initial impression was that it appeared little had changed since his last encounter with her.

Ashlyn was still a strikingly beautiful woman. Her long chestnut hair hung in waves down to her lower back when she didn't have it contained in a clip to give herself a more professional appearance. He recalled having been there when she'd run in and out of the bathroom experimenting with different hairstyles. *Was this too that or was this way better for this situation*…and so on. There was a confidence within her now that signified she no longer doubted herself. Her full lips and high cheekbones were as usual embellished with varying shades of rubies. Her blue eyes appeared to be more of a sensual grey, although at the moment they were looking at him warily, as if wondering why he'd chosen to accept a job protecting her when their last encounter had been nothing less than a mutual battleground.

Keane wasn't quite so sure of his reasoning either, but he'd have time to sort through his motivations later once he'd heard her story.

The small amber-colored throw on the arm of the leather couch clued Keane in that Ashlyn had spent a night or two here over the course of the last week. Otherwise, the knitted afghan would have been folded to perfection and put away in the bottom cabinet of her bookcase. She'd always liked things tidy. There could be more than one reason for that, actually. She'd had a habit of staying at work as she was nearing the end of an important case, kibitzing over minor details of the testimony prior to closing arguments. She was a creature of habit and he—unfortunately—knew a lot about her daily routines because he'd been one of them. Was that why her latest admirer had taken it upon himself to enter her home uninvited? Was he a recent eviction from her life? Had he missed her warmth after having grown accustomed to it like he once had? Or was this one drawn from the tide of humanity that she ignored each day on her trek through life?

Ashlyn had a headache or else the bottle of ibuprofen wouldn't still be sitting on her desk. The glass of water she'd used to swallow the pills was currently still half-full and positioned on the Edwardian side table sitting atop a stone coaster next to a Venetian crystal pitcher that most likely cost more than the simple black leather Boston dress shoes Keane was wearing. That point didn't really bother him. She was accustomed to the finer things in life, courtesy of being raised in a rather wealthy family. What concerned him was the offense she seemed to take at his appearance here in her little world.

The one thing that stood out to everyone present above all else was the look of surprise that was plastered across Ashlyn's face upon seeing him enter her office. It shouldn't have given Keane a sense of satisfaction that she hadn't been prepared for his presence, but it did. All he wanted to do to make the moment complete was to reach over to her and use one finger to pop her jaw back into place.

Agent Coulter had already stepped forward and shook hands with the two men currently standing in front of Ashlyn's desk. Both men introduced themselves before Ashlyn had a chance to walk back around her desk, albeit somewhat pale. Keane noticed the barely perceptual limp as she favored her left foot. It had only been two days since she'd called 911 upon discovering someone had been in her apartment and her wound still had to be quite tender. Leave it to her to wear those shoes today. She'd always worn heels if she had to appear in court or she would have changed into flats around the office. It appeared she hadn't had time to make that switch.

The police had doubted Ashlyn's timeline of the night, according to the tone evident in their report. They'd all had a rude awakening when it was verified that an unknown perpetrator was undeniably keeping tabs on a high profile federal prosecutor by hacking into her private security system. The fact was that whoever had breached the system had only been uncovered once the database logs on the security company's Oracle server were produced for the FBI Cybercrimes Division the next day. Now it was in Agent Coulter's hands and he'd gotten exactly nowhere in the thirty-six hours he'd had the case. It appeared Keane might be here a while, if all he was going to do was protect his former lover from a threat someone else was going to investigate.

Keane wasn't pleased with his new employer's track record

in the least. As a matter of fact, he'd been somewhat serious about that thirty-day probationary period once he'd discovered who his first client would be.

"Ashlyn, I'm sure Mr. Garner explained to you about the limits of the services he's contracted with SSI," Keane said, noticing the way she'd crossed her arms. She'd taken a defensive posture early on. She'd always had the tendency to be cold in air-conditioned rooms, but the chill to her soft skin had him wondering just how much this incident from the other night had rattled her. She was literally a block of ice. "Have there been any recent developments I should be made aware of?"

Keane had spent his flight going through the dossier that Calvert had so graciously provided, as well as having already briefly discussed the case with Coulter. There wasn't anything new to add to the investigation, but that didn't mean Ashlyn hadn't run into trouble since this morning. It was highly unlikely, considering Gina had said her employer had been in court all day as evidenced by the heels.

"No," Ashlyn responded, her gaze seeking out Agent Coulter's to reinforce her answer. "Unless something has happened that I'm not aware of. I haven't checked my email just yet."

"Unfortunately, nothing," Coulter replied, only to then remain intentionally silent after slipping his hands into the pockets of his matching suit slacks. It was apparent he wanted to speak with Ashlyn in private.

"Mr. Sanderson, give me a call if you need anything from our office," Jarod interjected, as if that checked off a box on his list of to-do things. Keane nodded as he took the man's business card, aware of how busy someone of Garner's high-ranking position could be. He slipped Garner's card into his wallet and produced his. Jarod's record was spotless; his family was somewhat a little too perfect on paper, and he had a reputation of getting things done. Keane was sure there were a few bodies in the family closets, but nothing to do with Ashlyn's case. "And please give Townes my regards when you speak with him. If you'll excuse me, I have an appointment I'm actually late for."

Jarod Garner took his leave, having already pulled out his cell phone to stare at the screen. It didn't go unnoticed that he'd been receiving multiple messages in the span of the three minutes they'd spoken. Victor Wright stayed behind, clearly not having picked up on Agent Coulter's intentional silence.

"I've taken a quick look at Ashlyn's home security system, as well as her private computer network," Victor professed, appearing to want to take a seat. He remained standing when no one else moved. "I've had my people modify what firewalls they could remotely and will replace some other vertical firewall logging preferences this evening. The permissions on the log access files were set to allow pretty much anyone to erase files. I thought you should know."

"I appreciate that," Agent Coulter said, surprisingly accepting of Victor's offer to do the enhancements. Keane speculated to himself as to why, especially after having indicated he'd cleared no one as a suspect…even those who worked closely with Ashlyn. "Would you please give us a private moment with Ashlyn?"

"Yes, yes, of course," Victor replied, finally having comprehended why there was a slight tension in the air. "Ashlyn, you're still okay with the changes we discussed?"

"Yes," Ashlyn conceded before addressing Victor. "But is there a chance you can stop by tomorrow morning, say around six-thirty? I'm going to be pulling a late night this evening and I really can't afford to—"

"About that," Agent Coulter interjected before Keane could intercede and voice his own objections. There were too many variables right now and as much as Ashlyn would like to work on whatever case she was currently prosecuting, there were more important things to deal with—like her personal safety. "I think it best if Victor is able to upgrade your systems this evening."

Ashlyn looked as if she was going to argue, but didn't as she took the time to study Coulter and his body language. She was used to doing so in the courtroom and Keane imagined she was fairly good at it with the suits she'd dealt with every day. She didn't disappoint when she slowly nodded her acceptance to the change in her schedule.

"Fine," Ashlyn replied deliberately, adding on a strained smile. "I'll let my staff know. Victor, what time works best for you this evening? Can I still use my network while you're logged into my system's preferences?"

"I'll need to bring one of my technicians to install some additional hardware, so it'll be roughly in around an hour and a half." Victor lifted an arm and looked at his watch as if to confirm. Keane was surprised Victor wasn't sporting one of those iWatch models out on the market now. The cyber unit chief gave a nod of verification before offering his hand to Agent Coulter. "I'll have a memorandum of what system changes we've done sent over to you immediately so you can forward the report to your cyber analysis team."

"Mr. Wright," Keane acknowledged, shaking the man's hand and noticing the firm grip once again. Victor was confident in himself, which wasn't surprising given his position. There hadn't really been anything about him in the report, but Keane would follow up with Brody to see if anything of note stood out in the man's background or his personal habits. "We'll see you shortly."

Keane didn't miss the way Ashlyn compressed her lips in displeasure, most likely directed at him down multiple avenues.

There were things they needed to discuss and he might as well set the ground rules early, but he wouldn't do so in front of Agent Coulter. Keane would allow the agent to make his request and then try to extinguish the sparks before they ever had a chance to spread like wildfire.

"Ms. Ellis, I'm sure you've already been notified by your paralegal regarding the results of today's investigations," Agent Coulter started out, walking closer to Ashlyn's desk and resting his hands on the back of the guest chair. "We found nothing here in your office, which lends itself to certain conclusions."

"Why are you making it sound as if that's a bad thing?" Ashlyn asked with her gaze solely on Coulter. She wasn't ready to deal with Keane and he completely understood her motivations. He'd had the entire plane ride to come to terms with their prior personal and future professional involvement. "We spoke about this yesterday morning. I don't think someone with this type of interest has anything to do with my work or the people I work with. It's most likely someone I might have run across in my apartment building, the cleaners or maintenance guys, or maybe the coffee shop I like to frequent. I'm not unaccustomed to reading people either, Agent Coulter."

"I'm not saying you aren't, but have you considered the individual we're looking for doesn't need to monitor you here? Whoever it is we're seeking has a very extensive knowledge of computer systems and technology in general. I believe we're looking for a male, most likely in his thirties due to the range of his experience at remaining undetected while conducting surveillance. I imagine it is also someone you've run into on more than one occasion and he's taken a simple gesture as something more than what you intended it to be. This isn't your average stalker, Ms. Ellis, and I believe your life could very well be in danger now that you've rejected his initial advances."

"Rejected him?" Ashlyn said those words as if warning the federal agent to continue. Keane pulled out the guest chair Garner had vacated earlier and took a seat, somewhat enjoying the developing scene before him. He'd thought of Ashlyn often over the years, missing her quick wit and the challenges he'd faced when debating with her over everyday things. She'd kept him on his toes those three months they'd been together and he could honestly say he'd missed it...not that he would ever tell her that in a month of Sundays. They'd had their chance to get it right and both had chosen to walk away. "You make it sound as if I've brought this on myself. I didn't invite this man into my home. I work at least sixteen-hour days, if not more. My job requires me to be on twenty-four hour call, because these cases your agents dig up don't prosecute themselves. Have I turned down invitations to dinner? Yes. Have I rudely rejected some guy? No. So I don't appreciate you making it seem as if I'm to blame for someone else's inability to accept no as an answer to his unwanted advance."

"Then let me rephrase," Agent Coulter countered, not backing down from the profiles he'd most likely gotten from the behavioral analysis unit on the perpetrator and one on Ashlyn herself. Keane casually reached out and took a mint from the crystal dish positioned near the corner of her desk. "The subject we're looking for believes he was rejected and we have no idea how he is going to react to the authorities being called in or the fact that you now have twenty-four hour protection, which will make it that much harder for him to gain access to you. I'm on your side, Ms. Ellis. We are not the enemy. We understand that you did nothing intentional to precipitate this individual's level of interest in you. He has most likely developed a warped sense of self and a corresponding lack of interpersonal coping skills due to some trauma in his life. You popped up on his scope somehow and he was determined you are worth his focus and affection as he knows it."

Ashlyn inhaled slowly as she backed down from the affront she'd sensed being made, regrouping and then motioning with her hand for Coulter to take a seat. He declined with a shake of his head. Keane moved the mint to the other side of his mouth as he waited out this terse discussion, not in any hurry to be up next in the batting cage. It was a test with her. Everyone got their turn sooner or later. *Only ten cents a try to knock the huge chip off of her shoulder*, he imagined the carnival caller shouting.

"I'll meet you and Mr. Sanderson at your apartment in thirty minutes. I'd like to bring some equipment I'll need into your apartment. This perp had a view of you in your office, as well as the front door. What he did not have is any audio or visual for the remaining space that we know of."

"But you think he might have had some," Ashlyn responded, slowly sitting down in her desk chair. Keane wanted to reassure her that she was safe from harm, but he couldn't do that. He wouldn't lie. There was no telling what lengths this individual would go to in order to be with her, as Coulter so clearly explained. "You also think it's a man instead of a woman and that he may have done this before."

"Yes."

"And you're suggesting it might be someone I work with here in the office?"

"I'm not ruling anyone out," Coulter said before he shifted his focus to Keane. "Thirty minutes. I want to be gone before Mr. Wright brings in his technician."

"Wait," Ashlyn objected, holding up a hand to halt the conversation. "You think Victor is—"

"I'm saying that I want to keep everything above board. Victor Wright is the head of your cyber division and it's only natural that your colleagues would want to assist you. It's not my intention to make anyone uncomfortable, but I will be having my fellow agent in the cyber unit monitoring your system. I highly doubt this suspect is going to just vanish after all the time and trouble he's taken to garner your attention. Just so you're aware, I've set up interviews with your staff through your assistant. I'll be conducting those discussions tomorrow morning."

"We'll be there in thirty minutes," Keane informed him, deliberately bringing this meeting to a close. He and Ashlyn had personal things to discuss before leaving this office and now it appeared they had a time constraint.

There was literally no sound as the FBI agent left. Keane turned his focus to Ashlyn, who was still looking at the door Coulter had just closed. She rested her French manicured nails on the hard surface in front of her and he wondered just how long she would allow time to pass before *actually* acknowledging him.

Keane didn't alter his expression when Ashlyn's blue eyes finally turned to him, as if his try in the barrel had arrived. She regarded him with what appeared to be caution as he paused a moment to think through what he was going to say. He had to remind himself to keep this professional, but the chance of that was nearing zero at the moment. She would always be personal to him.

"Townes Calvert thought it best if I took this case due to our previous involvement," Keane offered rather directly, not willing to prolong the awkward nature of this initial meeting. He stood and walked toward the window where she had her blinds open. He reached for the long string but didn't immediately pull the slats closed. He observed the disarray of the city street below, watching the traffic and pedestrians battle for the right of way as darkness finally descended. "Calvert assumed we have an established trust that will make this situation a bit easier, but you let me know if that isn't the case. I'm sure a replacement can be up here by tomorrow morning, and I can find better things to do. No problem."

Keane tried not to let it bother him when Ashlyn didn't reply right away, telling him she was actually considering the out he'd given her. He looked across the street, noticing the building and the easy access any number of people could gain to its upper floors and where she could be observed from that particular location should someone have the right equipment. He made a mental note to run that by Calvert and see if there was any cross-decking between these two municipal buildings. The one he was staring at was part of Judiciary Square and held the Juvenile Probation Office, among other things.

"I'm surprised you even agreed to come up here and take this meeting," Ashlyn said softly after clearing her throat. She'd certainly deflected answering the question nicely, but then again, she was rather proficient at that considering her profession. "The way things ended for us…"

Keane pulled the crisp nylon string, instantly enclosing them inside the office with a resounding snap of the blinds. The light inside took on an artificial and bland cast, matching the moods of those inside their own little bubble of gloom. The overhead illumination appeared stark now, reminding him to shed some of that light on their current, rather grim situation.

"You should know me well enough that I've always seen through any assignment given to me. That hasn't changed."

"*You've* changed."

"You haven't."

Keane didn't mean that as an insult, but rather a compliment; however, the comment had come so rapidly on the heels of her observations that it created a report as if a rifle had been fired. Ashlyn was just as beautiful now as she'd been five years ago, and he hated to see her wince at the crack. He sighed as he accepted that she wasn't going to take the out he'd given her to bail. Sometimes life wasn't fair for the home team. He'd have to suck it up and play.

"I can't afford to allow this to interfere with the case I'm currently prosecuting," Ashlyn said resolutely, nicely detouring away from their confrontation. She reached for the silver pen that had been lying on a folder. It was the same Mont Blanc Meisterstuck she'd used back when they'd been together. It had been her father's before hers. "Closing arguments will most likely take place at the end of the week. I need to prepare post haste."

"And you can," Keane assured her, not wanting to make her daily grind any harder than it had already become. The lines at the edge of her eyes betrayed the long hours she'd expended pursuing her dream. "I'm sure that Agent Coulter is more than capable of handling details of the case, and I'll be here to oversee your personal protection. Now is the time to tell me if there's anything I need to know that you might have kept to yourself out of some polite notion of embarrassment. Have you noticed anything unusual, especially recently? Was there any past liaisons that ended badly or a gentleman who propositioned you who you may have dismissed out of hand? Are there any high-profile cases that you prosecuted in the past few months that you feel could have something to do with this? Had anyone approached you in a threatening manner or that you found oddly casual for someone you didn't recognize?"

Keane would have added in a request for the names of men Ashlyn had ended intimate relationships with recently, but she might have taken that the wrong way. And according to what she'd just revealed to Coulter, she hadn't partaken in any extracurricular activities recently. He assumed that meant serious versus casual, and he personally understood her definition on both. He'd eventually have to clarify her statement to be sure.

Keane had the entire plane ride to digest the fact that he'd been put in an awkward situation. She'd had roughly ten minutes. He would give her time to catch her breath, and then he would ask the questions that would allow him to perform his job more effectively. He had to remind himself that he wasn't investigating who was causing her problems. He was only here to provide her protection.

"I'm sure you've already reviewed my caseload, as well as been given the names of people I see on a daily basis," Ashlyn countered evenly, watching Keane closely as he slowly crossed back across the room to take a seat in the chair that he'd just vacated in front of her desk. Her right brow was arched in the same manner as when she was questioning a defendant in court. "I assume you were given that list?"

"Yes, I was briefed."

"Then why inquire about things you already know the answers to?"

"You and I both know how this works. Information on paper gives a one-sided perspective of the situation in hand. I need your perspective of the ground."

"There have been no cases recently that would have warranted this kind of response, nor was there a defendant who assumed a casual manner with me," Ashlyn conceded, twirling the silver pen in her fingers as she looked down at the multiple files on her desk. Her lashes came close to touching her flushed cheeks as she then tapped the end of the writing utensil against the folders. "Before that, I spent eight months on a corporate healthcare fraud case that's taken up most of the media's time for the past year—of which I'm sure you are aware."

Ashlyn didn't need to spell it out for him. She'd sunk the majority of her time into prosecuting the defendants, leaving little to no personal hours to herself or anyone else. She'd always put one hundred and ten percent into everything she had to offer toward her profession. Again, proving his point that she hadn't changed her spots.

"How is this going to work between the two of us?" Ashlyn inquired softly, lifting her lashes to meet his narrowed gaze. Her blue eyes didn't blink as she waited for his answer.

"You're going to pack up what files you'll need for this evening," Keane responded, providing Ashlyn what she wanted. They'd each given their tremulous past the cursory words needed for the moment and now it was business only for the foreseeable future. He received the message loud and clear. He stood and adjusted his suit jacket, fastening the button to prevent the casual display of his concealed firearm in its black leather holster. "You're going to introduce me to your team of paralegals just before we walk out to the town car I hired for the duration of your protection detail. The driver has been vetted by my agency and is actually an old friend of Townes Calvert. We're going to start varying your routine and route to make it difficult to pinpoint your location at any given time."

"I have to prepare for closing arguments," Ashlyn warned, almost daring him to say that he was going to disrupt her efforts to do her job. She gently set down her pen and made no effort to choose which files she needed to go through this evening. "I'm not trying to make your task of protecting me harder, but I refuse to allow this man to get in the way of justice for the people our government represents."

Ashlyn stood and the small movement at the corners of her eyes indicated her injury was still sore. She reached hesitantly down toward her briefcase, not surprisingly the same one she'd used for many years, even before their time together. It wasn't a brand name or something flashy one might expect from a high-powered attorney like herself. It was a worn, brown leather case that was also her father's, given to her upon his retirement from the bench.

"You concentrate on doing your job and let me do mine," Keane reiterated as he looked over to the large round clock with Roman numerals. They were running a few minutes behind and he still needed to meet her staff. "We should be going ASAP."

Keane waited patiently while Ashlyn chose what files she would need. It was a wonder she could carry the briefcase by the time she was done piling them into the satchel. She'd been quiet and concentrating on the task at hand when she stopped just shy of clasping the flap.

"I'll understand if you want to call for someone else."

Ashlyn had spoken so softly that Keane had to strain to hear her. She hadn't addressed him in regret of what had happened, but more so in that she didn't want to cause him any more pain. Had this situation been presented to him three or four years ago, then maybe his anger for how she'd handled the end of their relationship would have factored into his decision. Now? He'd grown personally, most likely as she had, and he wouldn't allow past mistakes to get in the way of guarding her against a threat. That was his job. Besides, he'd already accepted he was to blame for their failed relationship as well. They both were guilty of neglect and ignoring the truth.

"There's no need. Not anymore." Keane reached for the briefcase, still unfastened. He made an effort to not to touch her as he secured the flap and then hoisted the bag off of the desk. It was then he chose to meet her questioning gaze. "We're both professionals, Ashlyn. Neither of us will make the mistake of crossing that line again."

CHAPTER SEVEN

A SHLYN STOPPED IN the middle of several cubicles, clearing her throat to capture the attention of her team of paralegals. It wasn't as if she'd needed to, considering that all of their eyes had been on the door to her office anyway. All four of them were well aware she'd been on the receiving end of someone's attention. Their body language dripped with anticipation. They were about to find out just how serious the problem had become and each would react as expected in such a situation.

The beige walls of their cubicles were waist high, allowing them to converse to one another without any impediments. There were thick volumes of transcripts, books, and various research means scattered on their desks—folders of every kind and color. The long table in the back held even more material, reminding her that they all had a lot of work ahead of them on a number of pending cases.

All Ashlyn wanted to do right now was a five-minute briefing. Her style of leadership fostered a free exchange of ideas, and she tried to keep the entire team up to speed on the latest developments whenever possible. The day she'd spent in court hadn't gone as she'd thought it would, with the judge issuing a presumptive ruling dismissing a vital piece of evidence based on the fact that the search of one of the defendant's computers hadn't been done legally according to the scope of the warrant. The search warrant hadn't included laptops that were subsequently discovered in the company vehicles. The defense argued successfully that the laptops were outside the purview of the warrant and had been swept up during the search illegally. The evidence that had been found on said drives was inadmissible due to being fruit of the poisoned tree. The final cherry on top of her cupcake had been having Keane walk into her office and stating he was her twenty-four seven protection for the foreseeable future.

It did dawn on her that she hadn't dwelt on what happened the other night in the midst of the most recent turmoil, with the exception of every time she had to stand for an extended period of time on her injured foot in these damned heels. She wanted nothing more than to get this horseshit decision overturned based on some sound research and good precedence in previous case law. To do that, she needed to hide away in her home office and pretend the ghost of relationships past wasn't taking up residence outside her apartment. She could do that once she immersed herself into writing her motion arguing that the original warrant included all company property including vehicles owned and operated to conduct said business.

"As you all know, the FBI was here earlier," Ashlyn said, once all eyes were on her. She remembered her internship as a paralegal back in the day and could appreciate all the hard work they put into their research and writing motions in support of her arguments. She treated them with respect, but she expected the same professional conduct as she'd expected of herself and she never socialized with them on a personal level. With that said, they did need to be kept apprised due to their involvement in her daily life and the fact that this could affect their access to her schedule, not to mention that each of them could expect an interview with the FBI. "A Special Agent Matthew Coulter is handling the case and he'd like to speak with each and every one of you tomorrow morning. I've already had Gina set up the schedule and she most likely has already forwarded it to you. My schedule might vary from my normal routine, so please check with Gina if you need to speak with me or call my cell."

"Is there anything specific we can do to help you, Ms. Ellis?" Mia asked, her gaze continually drifting toward Keane.

Ashlyn recognized her curiosity over concern. It didn't surprise her in the least, considering Mia had recently gotten engaged. One of the reasons she'd been hired for the last opening was due to her strong ethical and moral compass. This young girl would go far in her career.

"I appreciate the gesture, but the FBI should have this resolved very quickly," Ashlyn reassured her staff with half a smile reflecting her level of confidence. "I would like you to meet Keane Sanderson, an SSI agent. He'll be by my side until this is resolved as added personal protection. Keane, I would like you to meet Mia Hernandez, Aiden Young, Parker Davis, and Reed Foster. These are the members of my personal team."

Once the introductions were done, Ashlyn stepped back and allowed Keane to say a few words. He made a small joke, putting them at ease and reassuring them that it would be business as usual. He went over some precautions they'd most likely want to take with their own personal information and safety, as well as how they were to notify him if they suspected anything out of the ordinary or were approached by anyone suspicious. He hadn't changed much physically or professionally in the five years since they'd been together. He was still confident, blunt, and efficient among other things when it came to his job.

For the first time since Keane had set foot in her office, Ashlyn was able to really study him without his own intense observation. She was finally over the shock of seeing him back from the past, but she wasn't able to keep the memories of their time together from returning as if it hadn't occurred yesterday. The two of them had met three months before she received her current position as a federal prosecutor. She'd been in California at the time as a state's prosecutor, garnering trial experience and working a well-publicized case that had crossed multiple state lines.

The two of them had managed to find time to have dinner once in a great while and would grab a cup coffee if she'd had five minutes to spare, but it was their nights that were occupied by more than just words. Ashlyn had gone into the casual relationship knowing it would only be for the duration of her stay on the West Coast. Keane…well, he thought he was ready for more and that fateful day proved anything but. In the end, neither of them had been ready for something as serious as it had gotten.

"I think that covers everything," Keane finished up before turning the floor back over to Ashlyn. She forced another smile as the memories faded. "Is there anything else you'd like to add?"

"No," Ashlyn replied with a small shake of her head, emerging from her daze. All four set of eyes were directed on her and she straightened her shoulders so all they were able to see was encouragement. "I think that about does it. I'll be available by phone should anyone need me."

The look of surprise on her team's faces wasn't much of a revelation considering she was usually still in her office by the time these four had wrapped up their workday. It also didn't look good from the standpoint that closing arguments were only a few days away, provided that she was able to put her warrant issue to bed. It would be a long night for her whether she was at the office or working from home.

Ashlyn bid them goodnight, with a few instructions to Aiden to go over the transcripts thus far to confirm a few responses the defendant's counsel had answered concerning an earlier deposition. She wanted to confirm Glasson's reaction, though she did remember it clearly. Having an exact quote would only drive her point home with the jury.

They were walking through the elevator doors into the basement in under two minutes. Keane stayed close enough to her that the captivating fragrance of his cologne enveloped her, regardless that they had just stepped into the parking garage. The temperature had cooled quite a bit, which wasn't surprising since the weatherman had indicated they were due for some storms within the next couple of days. Night would have fallen outside and the streetlights would be on, casting a golden glow on the sidewalks. Ashlyn had turned her face away from the yawning garage bay before them when she realized Keane was observing the area as he continued to escort her to a town car not thirty feet away. They didn't make it far when her name was called out and Keane immediately shielded her body with his.

"Ashlyn, do you have a—" Andrew Rutledge stopped short in confusion, most likely not even aware of what had taken place over the last few days. The Haung case was very high profile and he'd been working around the clock. "I'm sorry. I didn't mean to interrupt."

"It's fine, Andrew," Ashlyn replied with a reassuring smile, peering around Keane's silhouette. She immediately realized the way Keane had turned into her must have seemed like a rather intimate gesture. She'd even raised her hand and placed her palm on Keane's chest, so she instantly tried to step away. He didn't make it easy. "Was your assistant able to clear your calendar before lunch tomorrow?"

Ashlyn had run into Andrew on her way to court this morning, but she hadn't had time to speak with him. They'd taken the
shuttle together over to the courthouse and she'd been too busy
reviewing the questions she was going to ask her witness on the
stand. Gina had no doubt already contacted his assistant and set
up a meeting for tomorrow, but Ashlyn would confirm that now.

"Unfortunately, I can't meet in the morning," Andrew replied, shifting his briefcase to his other hand as he pulled out his
cell phone. He dismissed whoever was calling by silencing his
phone. "Do you have time in the afternoon?"

"I'll be in court." Ashlyn's schedule was tight this week and
there might not be a moment where she could give her opinion
on the direction of his case. "Have you tried Bishop? He seems
to have a lot of time on his hands nowadays."

"Yeah, I heard he was trying to make it worth Mia's while to
switch teams." Andrew grimaced with what appeared regret and
then shrugged his shoulder. The lights from the building made
the fabric of his suit jacket appear darker. "I never did like the
way he does business and there isn't a snowball's chance in hell
I'll take his advice on the Haung case. Listen, just call me if you
get a moment."

Ashlyn only nodded, her thoughts now distracted by the fact
that Bishop Vance was going after one of her paralegals. Why?
He had his own team and there wasn't any reason for him to
poach from hers. Andrew walked back into the building and it
occurred to her that he never asked who Keane was or made an
effort to make introductions. His mind was on other things and
now so was hers…Keane's hand was still resting on her lower
back.

"If it helps any, I don't think I'm in any physical danger."
Ashlyn wasn't downplaying what had been happening to her by
any stretch of the imagination. She certainly didn't like the

unwanted attention, and though his escalation had her worried…it seemed as if it was just an overblown infatuation. She'd stepped forward and Keane stayed close. She hadn't had anyone in her personal space in quite a while. "What I mean is, I don't think he wants to hurt me. Yes, he's upset I'm not returning his interest and he needs to be confronted before he—"

"Kidnaps and rapes you?" Keane asked, taking the liberty to finish her sentence. Only he'd turned the tables on her and used it against her. She adjusted the straps on her purse in frustration. "Kills you?"

The garage had been somewhat cleared by the earlier rush hour, but the night was just beginning outside. Music from the bars and restaurants nearby on the block could be heard from above, while annoying horns still blaring could be heard in protest as everyone vied for their spot in the slow flow of traffic. The various sounds weren't enough to prevent her from hearing Keane's warning though.

"You and I both know how a person can escalate over the most innocent of gestures…a wave of your hand. This perp went from emails to watching you in the privacy of your own home over your laptop camera. He went to the trouble to find a way to touch your personal belongings…probably to watch you while you slept. That's beyond an infatuation, Ashlyn. I'd say that establishes an escalating, rather unhealthy obsession, wouldn't you?"

Ashlyn had only meant that Keane shouldn't have to feel as if the sight of a weapon was trained on them every time they were in public. He'd had enough of that with his time in the military. Did he think she was naïve? Of course she understood just how severely her situation had spiraled out of control. She'd been the one living it for the last three months and it certainly hadn't been a bed of roses. Whenever she thought of a man watching her sleep, eat, or even shower, she immediately became physically ill. Did he really think this man would try to hurt her the next time?

Ashlyn just barely prevented herself from snapping back at him. It certainly wouldn't help the situation and the tension between them was thick enough as it was. Agent Coulter had the best of the best working with him in the government sector. It shouldn't take long to locate whoever had been stalking her and then Keane would be able to go back to...exactly where was he working out of now? Jarod had mentioned that SSI was located in Florida. She hadn't been aware that Keane had moved there.

"What about my vehicle?" Ashlyn asked, changing the subject as they stepped up to the driver of the town car. The man was currently holding her door open for her and she gave him an appreciative smile. He was of average height, average build, and average appearance. He blended in well, especially to those residents of D.C. "Thank you."

"You're quite welcome, ma'am."

"Ashlyn, meet Jack. He'll be with us for the duration."

"It's nice to meet you, Jack," Ashlyn responded before Keane saw to it that she was safely inside the vehicle before she'd had the chance to shake Jack's hand. The interior was set to a comfortable temperature and she moved to the outer seat when it became evident Keane would be riding in the back of the car with her. "You could have at least allowed me the courtesy of telling him I need to stop at an ATM. I—"

Ashlyn realized she had never turned on the ringer to her phone since her time in court today when she felt the vibrations through the leather of her purse. She wasn't like Jarod and able to postpone answering, especially with all the irons in the fire she had at the moment. She'd already recognized the single pulsation as a text message before pulling out her lifeline to her job.

"My bank is—" Ashlyn had been going to give Jack a location when her gaze landed upon the small screen. Some people had the preview of their text turned off so no one could see the incoming message. Not her. She needed to be able to see information coming through without breaking stride. Her movements stilled as she read the warning she'd just been given. It was like the air had been knocked from her lungs, but she managed to whisper. "It seems I need to retract my earlier statement."

Keane indicated to Jack that he should immediately pull away toward the exit from the garage, having already noted the tremor in Ashlyn's voice. She couldn't help but look around them at the parking area, trying to catch sight of who might be responsible. Was *he* standing in the shadows? Was *he* watching them from his vehicle in the rows of cars? Was *he* even near them?

Ashlyn was no longer comfortable. A chill had invaded her suit jacket and her fingers had gone slightly numb as Keane held out his hand for her phone. She was finally able to get her tight grip to release the square device as she pulled her gaze from the vehicles left behind.

The lines around Keane's mouth tightened and his eyes darkened in response to what he read on the small screen. It didn't appear that he took pleasure in being right, but it did seem as if bringing in the FBI had been the exact trigger to produce an emotional response from the man Agent Coulter was searching for.

All Ashlyn wanted now was to be in the comfort of her own home…but that had been invaded too. She was starting to understand just how people reached a breaking point after some nutcase slowly chipped away at their defenses until they broke down. What *he* said in the text message wasn't true, but it was

Agent Coulter's job to make sure it couldn't happen.

"You are mine. You always have been. We'll be together soon."

HE CURLED HIS *lip in disgust and contempt.*

He'd wanted to see her facial expression when she received his text, but she'd been rushed into the backseat of the town car. Did she think one man could keep another such as him from claiming what was his?

No. This wasn't her fault. She was being used by weaker men.

She'd smiled at him today. She recognized their bond as he had.

The affection was her way of telling him someone had forced her to bring in the authorities. He could read her body language like no other. She wanted him to save her from those telling her what to do, forcing her to test the truth of his devotion.

He would now clear a path to their future.

CHAPTER EIGHT

K EANE CLOSED AND locked the deadbolt installed in the
door of Ashlyn's apartment behind him, noting that the
locks had been changed recently with a high quality replacement
set. He glanced at the casement and noted the heavy brass strike
box for the deadbolt. The next intruder would need considerable
better lock picking or bumping skills to negotiate that minefield
of security pin tumblers—unless, of course, he'd used a key.

What he was not surprised by was the faint scent of lavender
that hung in the air. It had been her favorite fragrance in the
candles she'd preferred to have in her home, not that he'd ever
been here before. She'd purchased a couple for the hotel room
where she'd stayed during that high-profile case for those few
months in California, opening up to him about her likes and
dislikes.

Keane had thought he'd known what to expect when he'd
walked through the front door, but all it did was remind him that
he really didn't know her at all. Their time together was a
microcosm of her world—representative but not all encompass-
ing, as he would soon find out.

Ashlyn had already crossed the small entryway and started to
turn right onto the grey slate of her kitchen. The modern
stainless steel appliances, along with the Divani white-leathered

tall chairs, were strikingly different than the antiquated worn oak office furniture she used at work. Keane immediately reached out and wrapped his fingers around the cuff of her suit jacket. She'd been quiet since receiving the text and that was understandable. He'd been on the phone with Coulter for the majority of the ride to her apartment building, but he wasn't about to let her wander around her apartment until he'd cleared the place of any immediate threats.

"Let me have a look around first, please," Keane said in a reassuring tone, motioning for her to stay by the front door. It hadn't been his intention to worry her any further, but her blue eyes creased in the corners indicating he'd done just that. He set her briefcase on the table to his left. "I won't be very long."

Keane walked past a thin side table up against the wall of the foyer. It was clear of the vase that had once been there, at least from what the initial crime report had detailed. He prevented himself from directing her to take off her heels, knowing how sore the cuts had to be after standing on her feet all day. He refrained though. Her comfort wasn't his place to manage any longer.

The apartment had an open layout, making it easier for him to ascertain risks. Her living room consisted of what looked like Brazilian hardwood flooring. A rather large white sheepskin rug lay in the middle of the contemporary furniture arrangement, consisting of a low-seated leather sectional with a couple of grey pillows to bring out the flooring in the kitchen. At least, that's what he thought she was going for. It was hard for him to picture her living in a place right off the cover of a design magazine, for that's what this appeared to be.

Keane could see an open arch at the other end of the apartment leading to what seemed to be her office. He chose the small hallway on his left first, calculating correctly that it would lead to her bedroom. Now this décor matched her personality better.

The rich color of burgundy in various shades was strewn throughout the room, from the comforter and pillows on her king-sized bed to the long curtains that were currently closed to prevent prying eyes from seeing inside of her sanctuary. Her bedroom furniture was dark cherry.

The bedroom and master bath weren't disturbed and Keane quickly made his way back down the short passageway. Ashlyn was standing in the foyer with her high heels in one hand and her purse in the other. He figured it wouldn't take long for her to remove the shoes to stand on the cold foyer floor and enjoy a bit of relief. A strand of her chestnut hair had come loose and it was obvious that her previous anxiety was slowly turning to anger.

Good.

Keane didn't like the thought of this lowlife scum causing Ashlyn to be afraid of her own shadow. She'd always been a rather strong-willed woman. This situation wasn't going to be the one thing that brought her down. They had a lot to talk about personally, but now wasn't the time as he needed to finish his sweep.

It didn't take Keane long to search the rest of Ashlyn's apartment. He took a look at her office, the small half-bath attached to it, along with what appeared to be a storage closet. Everything appeared in place. It was then that he started to study her security system as he made his way back to the main area.

No wonder Ashlyn's pursuer had tapped into her computer. There were no internal video cameras to allow this deviant scumbag to obtain a visual of her office, just as Coulter had said. The only surveillance camera Keane located was in the living room to monitor the front entrance from across the room. He began to get an uneasy feeling about where Coulter was taking this.

"We're clear," Keane called out, making his way back down the hallway to where Ashlyn had now walked back into the kitchen. She no longer had her shoes and purse in hand. "Agent Coulter should be here any minute."

"Let's hope the cyber unit he's working with found something useful," Ashlyn added on, sounding somewhat agitated. She hadn't even bothered to look around, telling him that Coulter's reason for actually stopping by wasn't on her mind. "How is it someone can send a text message and the world's best cyber technicians can't figure out who's sending it? I mean, everything this man has done has been through technology of some sort—my security feeds, my computer, my phone. I—"

"Not everything," Keane gently reminded her as he took off his suit jacket. He draped it over the back of one of the chairs. He would have suggested Ashlyn do the same, but he'd seen her like this numerous times in the past…although it had always been about the court case she'd been working on at the time. Nothing had really changed, and yet everything in their lives was different from their own perspectives. He pushed the thoughts of the past to the side. "He made his way into your home at some point. It's my job to figure out how and keep it from happening again."

"Don't you mean Special Agent Coulter?"

"No. It's his responsibility to locate the person doing this. Mine is to ensure your personal safety at all times."

Keane could see that Ashlyn wanted to know exactly why he'd accepted this assignment considering their past relationship and its rocky ending, but he was grateful when she didn't ask. Yes, he could have blatantly told Calvert that there wasn't a chance in hell he was going to travel to D.C. to protect a woman who'd made it plain that she'd wanted nothing further to do with him after summarily ending their brief affair in such an uncaring and cool manner. He didn't…and that gave him pause.

"How do you think he got in here?" Ashlyn asked, choosing to continue along this professional route Keane had put them on. She turned around and hit the brew button on her coffee machine a little harder than necessary. Again, it didn't surprise him to know she'd had it all set up and ready to go for when she needed it. He imagined her rinsing out the coffee pot, measuring out the grinds into the brass filter, and filling the reservoir with water just to leave it for later when she got home. She opened one of the cupboards and started to bring down two mugs.

"Even the police couldn't figure that out. There were no prints other than mine on my dresser. The doors were locked as if he'd never been here."

"Which is why you had the locks changed," Keane reminded her, pulling out his cell phone with every intention of calling Brody. The apartment building had security feeds and though the police and Coulter most likely had already gone through the footage, maybe there was something they were all missing. "Someone could have easily taken the keys from your office desk drawer and made a copy. I noticed you retrieved them when we left your office."

"Then you do think it's someone I work with," Ashlyn pushed him to confirm something he wouldn't divulge. The pool of suspects was too wide.

"I didn't say that. You ride the shuttle to the courthouse, you stop in at the coffee shop, and I'm sure there were other times when someone could have easily have lifted your keys from your purse. With the right molding, the ridges of a key are easy enough to replicate for a bump key."

It was going to take a group effort to find whoever had taken an unhealthy interest in Ashlyn. Plus, Keane wanted Brody to take a quick look into the paralegals, Garner, and Wright. These types of cases usually weren't random. It wasn't likely someone off the street had taken notice of her and gone this far. Ashlyn had crossed paths with this perp somewhere for him to be able to copy the key to her front door. She was a creature of habit. Work, home, repeat. Learning her routine wouldn't have taken too long, but it would have required more than a random encounter.

"I'm beginning to think new expensive locks won't be able to keep this man out," Ashlyn said softly, resting her palms on the granite counter in front of her. She lowered her head as if to compose herself. Keane unbuttoned the cuffs on his dress shirt to give him something to do other than reach for her. It wasn't his place. Old habits died hard. "So what now?"

"You do what you would normally do," Keane suggested, itching to go search for what he believed to be a hidden camera inside of Ashlyn's bedroom. He continued to roll up his sleeves as other possibilities made themselves known, but he'd wait for Coulter. "I'll do what I'm paid to do. If you could direct me to your step stool, I'll take care of the rest."

Ashlyn finally turned to face him, her innate need to argue that sentiment falling short of her lips. He could see the internal struggle she was dealing with, knowing full well he would get his way. Her devotion to her career had always come first and now would be no exception.

"Fine. The stool is in the closet." Ashlyn gave a curt nod and then cut through the other side of the kitchen to where she had most likely placed her shoes and purse. Sure enough, Keane caught sight of her as she made her way through the small entrance. "I'm going to change before I—"

A knock sounded on the door before Ashlyn had taken two

steps toward her bedroom.

"I'll get that," Keane said, motioning for her to stop. He didn't want her going into her bedroom right now. "Why don't you wait to change until after we meet with Coulter? I don't want to keep him waiting, especially since he'd like to be gone before Victor arrives."

Keane quickly sent a text message to Brody with the names of the people needing a background check. It would most certainly raise some red flags, but Calvert had enough pull in these political circles to see that the ruffled feathers were soothed. Keane added a quick note requesting the apartment building's security footage before confirming who was at the door prior to answering.

"Coulter," Keane greeted the agent, looking over the other gentleman who accompanied him. The tall, thin man was carrying a small black duffel bag. "Anything on the text message?"

"Nothing. Probably cloned the guy's phone while he was at lunch or waiting for the bus," Coulter responded after shaking Keane's hand and then doing the same with Ashlyn. Well, the agent's response wasn't exactly what Keane wanted to hear at the moment, but this case had various revolving parts that didn't seem to want to slow down any. "It was a local day worker's phone and somehow the perpetrator managed to ping the text off every cell tower available in the city. Ashlyn, this is Special Agent West. He'll be conducting the search we spoke of earlier."

West didn't waste time and immediately walked into the living room and placed the black duffel bag on the sofa. He began to lay out specialized equipment cases and specific devices onto the fabric, never once breaking stride as Ashlyn crossed her arms in defense of what was taking place. Her shoes still hung from her right hand. Keane could only imagine how violated she was feeling at the moment, most likely knowing very soon she would have confirmation someone had been watching her in other areas besides her kitchen and office.

"Would you like some coffee?" Ashlyn asked, not making any move to go into the kitchen. Keane could see she was taking a moment to strengthen her resolve. "I'm brewing some now."

"No, thank you," Agent Coulter replied, watching his colleague closely. "We'd like to get this done quickly. Why don't you grab yourself a cup while we finish up?"

Keane stepped forward before thinking, taking Ashlyn's shoes from her hand. The gesture didn't go unnoticed, although not by her. Holding a woman's heels conveyed intimacy and he didn't miss Coulter's raised eyebrow. Ashlyn was already making her way into the kitchen while warily watching West initiate the search of her apartment, who seemed unaware of the exchange and oblivious to the fact that other people were even present in the house.

"Let me know what you find," Keane directed, unwilling to address Coulter's interest.

Keane set Ashlyn's high heels underneath one of the stools before walking around the small island. She was pouring both of them coffee into the mugs she'd taken down from the cabinet, not a tremor to be seen. He should have known better than to be worried, but it came naturally to him. She set the glass carafe back onto the burner before sliding one of the cups over to him.

"You think they'll find something?"

"Yes." Keane wouldn't sugarcoat anything. She wouldn't appreciate it if he did. "I do."

Ashlyn visibly swallowed her disgust before raising the coffee to her lips. She washed down the revolting taste and then turned to watch the two agents do their job. She was trying her best to compartmentalize what was happening, but it wasn't always easy when the crime she fought every day of her life invaded the privacy of her own home.

Keane could easily relate. He wanted nothing more than to be able to do the grunt work and track this son of a bitch down himself. He hadn't thought it would be this hard to stay on the sidelines and just protect the primary. Isn't this what he'd wanted though—a simpler, easier day-to-day routine?

"I wasn't aware you'd moved to Florida," Ashlyn said softly, keeping the topic of discussion between them. Maybe she had caught Coulter's reaction. Most likely, she wanted to talk about anything other than what was taking place in her home. She turned and leaned up against the counter as she observed the two agents canvass her personal space. "Do you like it down there with all that sun and sand?"

"That's a good question," Keane responded, joining her as he positioned himself to face Coulter and West. They disappeared from view and walked into Ashlyn's bedroom. "I'm not quite sure yet. The fact of the matter is...I moved there this morning. At least my stuff did."

"Jarod Garner mentioned SSI was a new contractor, but I didn't realize he'd meant within the last few days." Ashlyn had one arm crossed over her middle as she stared at the piece of drywall that was preventing her from seeing into the hallway. Keane had a better view from where he was, but he imagined they wouldn't see the two agents for another few minutes. "Why the change?"

Those three words had more meaning in them than just mere conversation. Keane's desire to stay in California and the calling he'd had for his position on the SWAT team had been a small piece of what had gone wrong with their brief affair. Three months. It wasn't enough to get Ashlyn out of his system. He'd ended up wanting more, but she hadn't been willing to give up her goals and dreams of being a federal prosecutor after finishing up her stint as the state's hired hitwoman. No one had been to blame for the bad timing of their relationship, but it was the cruel, passionate response to ending something so beautiful that had tarnished the special time they'd spent together.

"I guess I finally wanted something more than what southern California offered," Keane answered honestly and not only to her. "I spent twelve years in the military, serving two combat tours, tearing up my mind and body. I probably should have finished the eight years to claim my retirement, but I was mentally too tired. It was my body that craved the adrenaline rush and LAPD SWAT gave me that without the physical toll of combat. It was like an addiction that finally faded. Let's face it— I'm thirty-seven years old. I deserve a little R&R and some peace of mind."

Keane didn't have to spell it out for Ashlyn. Had they met years after his return to the States, their relationship most likely would have endured her transition to D.C. He would have picked up his stakes and planted them in wherever. She hadn't been just one of many relationships. There was something about this woman that had nothing to do with her beauty—whether it was her intelligence, conviction, or morality he didn't know— and there wasn't a day he hadn't thought of her since.

Unfortunately, it had ended and they'd both gone on with their lives.

"The things I said..."

Keane lifted a corner of his mouth in a half smile of forgiveness, knowing full well Ashlyn didn't like to apologize. It wasn't in her nature. It meant that she'd been wrong and that so rarely occurred. He was very much that way as well, which was most likely one of the reasons their relationship had imploded. Neither had been willing to give up what they'd had at the time.

Ashlyn hadn't been the only one to say things they'd wished they could take back. They'd hurled hurtful words at each other, purposefully wanting to ricochet the pain they had experienced onto one another. He'd been no better than she, but nothing they said now could get those five years back.

"We were both too—"

"May I speak with you out in the hallway?" Coulter asked, not really waiting for their answer. He continued to the front door and simply walked out, knowing they would follow. Keane turned slightly so that he could set his coffee mug on the counter. He then physically took Ashlyn's when she hadn't so much as moved an inch. Her manicured fingers curled into tiny fists as she moved before he could put his hand on her lower back. Coulter didn't speak until the door had closed behind them, leaving them alone in the hallway. "It's my recommendation that the two of you stay somewhere else. The equipment we found in your bedroom and bathroom isn't your five-and-dime variety surveillance equipment. A lot of money has gone into watching every move you make, Ashlyn. There's no telling what this individual will do now that you're purposefully preventing him from realizing his goal."

Coulter didn't need to spell it out for them. Keane straightened for what he knew would be a battle. Ashlyn's first instinct would be to stay and defy that this man had become more than just dangerous—he was now lethal and she was in his crosshairs.

"No."

"I don't think you understand," Coulter countered, trying to reason with a woman who had already made her personal stand. Keane rubbed his jaw in total doubt the man would be able to get more than three words in before Ashlyn put a stop to the line that would lead to a roller coaster ride she didn't want to take. She didn't understand she was already in the car. "You—"

"I understand perfectly," Ashlyn stated evenly, squaring her shoulders and pointing to her front door. "That is my home. Mine. Not his and no one else's. I refuse to be put out by some pervert with a personality disorder. Destroy whatever you find, or better yet, take it with you as evidence and use it to track this son of a bitch down. SSI has hired Keane to protect me and he'll do just that while you do your job of finding out who has been watching me every minute of my day. So please, Special Agent Coulter, clear my home office of any threats so that I can do my job in putting away three men involved with the illegal distribution for sale of child pornography which has ruined sixteen children's lives."

Ashlyn opened the door to her apartment, leaving it standing wide open as she made her way to her bedroom without a backward glance. West had to move to the side in order for her to pass, but the action didn't faze him as he continued to run what looked like a baton across all the furniture in the living room.

"You need to get her to see reason." Coulter held up a disabled video lens with various wires dangling from the end. "There were multiple cameras positioned around her bedroom and master bathroom. I don't need to tell you how these cases escalate quickly. We've just removed the one thing that's given him some measure of satisfaction. He's already changed his course of action by texting her, reaching out to her personally instead of through anonymous letters and gifts. He most certainly has compromising video images of her which he could do anything with in an attempt to blackmail her or influence her behavior."

"We're also dealing with someone who is high-profile," Keane countered, not truly arguing what Coulter was saying, but wanting the agent to understand just how far reaching this case could go in the media. "Ashlyn's father was a federal judge with a reach that can stretch to the entire political stratosphere. He's a household name and you can bet your ass that some reporter isn't sitting on the sidelines waiting for a press briefing to update them on a case that was made to appear as if it was nothing of any significance. Should she step away from this case, someone is going to connect the dots and this scumbag is going to become notorious. That isn't a route we want or should take, but I will make a call in to my team and tell them that reinforcements are needed on the ground now. We'll have every entrance and exit point covered, along with extra security when traveling. We will electronically seal this place up so you couldn't tell the difference from an Amish farmhouse."

"I've already had the privilege of speaking with her father," Coulter admitted, palming the black camera and looking past Keane's shoulder. Someone was walking their way. "I don't like having to deal with politics in any of my cases, but we were both hired to do our jobs regardless of our personal preferences. I just don't want to have to finish up mine where my victim ends up dead."

"I didn't say you were wrong in giving your advice, just as you did." Keane looked over his shoulder to see a man entering his apartment three doors down before glancing to the apartment across from Ashlyn's. There was about to be a change in this complex's tenants. "As the saying goes, it's always better to know the ground prior to a battle. We're going to need all the advantages we can get."

CHAPTER NINE

"VICTOR AND NOAH just punched out. Your security system should now be state of the art, hands down the toughest system to crack."

Ashlyn looked up from the laptop and multiple file folders she had opened on her desk to find Keane leaning against the doorframe of her home office. She'd literally shut out all thought of what was taking place in her apartment as she focused on writing her motion to allow the files found on the laptops discovered in the company vehicles.

She had found numerous instances in case law that supported her conclusion that the company vehicles parked on the property leased by the corporation and used solely for business purposes should be recognized as included in the scope of the original warrant. Therefore, the judge could reverse his presumptive ruling and allow the evidence collected from those drives into evidence.

Ashlyn had emailed her assistants instructing them to write a brief that cited each of the cases she'd indicated and their relevance to her argument for the court's review tomorrow morning. Work was the only way she could escape the terrible feeling of violation she felt deep down inside when she'd seen the tiny camera lens that Agent Coulter had shown her. The job was the only way for her to get through to the other side, or else the fear would take over and she'd be frozen in this seat crying her eyes out.

"Who's Noah?" Ashlyn asked to give her something else to focus on besides the fact she now wanted nothing more than to move away from the scene of the crime. That wasn't an option though. She refused to be afraid in her own home. "I'm surprised he didn't bring Paul. He's always been our go-to guy at the office."

"Noah installed additional hardware for the security system, whereas Paul Bostle's experience lies in the software applications," Keane explained, crossing his arms as if he were settling in for a conversation. He didn't seem to understand that she wasn't ready to deal with their past either. Every time she heard his voice from the other room, it brought back memories of their time together. She'd wavered countless times with her urges to contact him after she'd left California for D.C. She hadn't been ready for a serious commitment then and wasn't in a much better position now. Why, then, had she felt as if she'd made a mistake? Was it the way it had ended? Why was she still feeling that way? "There's no need to worry. I've run background checks on both of them, but we'll still keep a close eye on anyone having anything to do with this system upgrade and computer access to your CPU and network hardware."

It was bad enough to believe someone had hacked into her security feeds and laptop computer camera, but it was something else entirely to realize she'd been observed every minute of every day for at least the last month or more. What if this man had been watching her longer than that? Had he been coming and going from her apartment every day without her realizing it? Her stomach rolled with nausea and all she could do was nod her head.

"I've given a team member from SSI the IP address of your router and the administrator password. He'll be keeping a close eye for anyone who tries to break into the system. He'll also be watching all network traffic with an Enterprise Network Monitor." Keane was still wearing his suit, sans the jacket. It was apparent he'd been running his hands through his hair from the way the waves were disrupted and Ashlyn wondered if there was something he was keeping from her. She wanted nothing more than to ignore what was happening so she could bury herself in her work. "I understand why you're resistant to Special Agent Coulter's suggestion regarding staying elsewhere for the time being, but you'll have no other option should something else occur that would place your life in danger."

Ashlyn leaned back in her chair and closed her eyes, not comfortable with any of this. How could she be? This guy was prying into her life with a jackhammer.

"Do you still have a headache?"

"How did you know I had a headache?" Ashlyn asked, lifting her lashes to see Keane hadn't moved from the doorway.

Keane was still watching her closely and it made her antsy, causing her to rethink the way she was dressed. She'd changed into her favorite pair of sweatpants she'd had since her law school days, her beloved warm fuzzy socks, along with a long-sleeved black shirt that was made of the smooth material she loved. She'd gone without a bra for comfort's sake, but was second-guessing that decision now. Her nipples had to imprint clearly through the soft material and she suspected that her breasts moved just enough to garner his attention. She kept an arm on the desk in a manner that it laid in front of her, blocking his view. She decided it would be better if she went to her bedroom to put on a bra.

"You had a bottle of ibuprofen out on your desk at the office. You also haven't eaten dinner, so your electrolytes are running low and your blood pressure will be up."

The thought of eating had Ashlyn's stomach lurching once again, so she slowly shook her head in response. She'd removed her hair clip but had piled her hair loosely on top of her head in a band. It tightened with her movements and she curbed a wince. She still had hours of work ahead of her and had yet to even open her email to go over the notes Mia, Aiden, Parker, and Reed had sent over. All four of them had put in a late night, which wasn't unusual, but she would normally have gone over their material by this time and provided some relevant feedback. At the rate she was going, she would have to pull another all-nighter.

"I'm fine," Ashlyn replied with her standard answer with a not too convincing smile. She reached forward for her pen and opened another folder, this one containing interviews of the men who'd paid for the services the defendant had offered. Her headache became worse at the testimony she was about to review. "Thank you for handling the security system and the support people while I continued to work."

"It's what I'm here for," Keane replied, although she was certain there was sarcasm lacing his tone. Ashlyn hadn't meant for her gratitude to sound dismissive. "Paul was able to update your computer network via remote access through the router, but he disabled the video camera connected to the security system as a precaution. I'll be in the living room should you need anything."

Ashlyn glanced over at her laptop monitor where a small yellow sticky note was currently covering the lens, but Keane was gone before she could tell him she'd taken her own extra precautions. She sighed in resignation of just how out of control her life had become in a span of forty-eight hours. Yes, it had been much longer than that, but she'd still been in control of how she did things daily. Now? She had no idea what to feel or how to act, so she did what she did best. She withdrew into herself and concentrated solely on the case in front of her.

Ashlyn glanced at her office phone, wishing it wasn't going on midnight. Her father was usually the first person she called when things went sideways, but she'd already called him once today about what was taking place. She assured him everything was under control now with the FBI hot on the trail and a full-time personal security guard. He and her mother were currently in Italy for their thirtieth wedding anniversary and there was no need to worry them needlessly, yet he'd informed her that he was going to make a few calls back home. Things were being taken care of and there wasn't anything further that either of her parents could do, other than hover. She ignored the impulse of calling them and forced herself to focus on the work at hand.

The next two hours passed slowly, but Ashlyn had been able to finally get a substantial start to her closing arguments, which she would need rather quickly if the defense rested after her motion was heard and ruled on. The defendant was currently taking the stand and questioning would resume tomorrow, but she highly doubted he would say anything to incriminate himself, having been prepped so well by his attorney. She honestly hadn't thought of anything else beyond listing the facts of the case to convey to the jury there was only one decision that made sense and justice needed to be served to protect the weakest of society. She recognized that her ability to do so was due to Keane's presence and the cocoon of security he was providing.

Ashlyn pushed him from her thoughts, trying to find the rhythm she'd been writing to, but finally admitted that it was gone. Once the genie had escaped the bottle, trapping the elusive miscreant was next to impossible. Maybe Keane's presence wasn't such a good thing. She rubbed her eyes and willed herself to concentrate by focusing on the evidence that had been ruled as admissible and that she could include in her summary. After rewriting the same sentence three times, she gave up.

It was then that Ashlyn realized the silence had become rather deafening. She could literally hear the grandfather clock from the other side of her apartment. Had Keane fallen asleep on her couch? He'd traveled from Florida and then hit the ground running, so she could only imagine how exhausted he must be. She'd converted the spare bedroom into her office, so the only place he had to camp out was her sofa. She winced at how uncomfortable that must be, considering she hadn't been the one to pick it out. It was purely for looks.

Months of living and breathing work hadn't given Ashlyn a lot of time to focus on her apartment, until one day Gina had stopped by with some files Ashlyn had forgotten at the office. She'd looked aghast at the empty space filled with unpacked boxes and it wasn't two days later that Ashlyn's home had been unpacked, filled with furniture, and designed to someone else's specifications. The thing of it was, she didn't mind it because she was rarely here. She also never socialized here. The only room she'd taken time to do herself had been her bedroom, and only because she hadn't been able to sleep with the white walls, modern art, and a lamp that resembled something from a sci-fi movie. Design by accident had been her comment at the time. Her loss of sleep lately had nothing to do with décor.

Ashlyn strained to hear any sounds of Keane inside of her apartment when it dawned on her that she hadn't seen him bring up a suitcase of any kind. Did he even have clothes to change into? A toothbrush? It wasn't her place to worry about what he had or didn't have, but she couldn't prevent herself from wheeling her chair back and crossing the hardwood floor to look out over the living room. He hadn't closed the door after checking on her earlier, so she quietly crossed the threshold. The lights were still on in the apartment.

"Everything okay?"

Ashlyn jumped at the rich sound of his voice, immediately finding him sitting on the leather couch. He was leaning forward and working on a laptop, although all his attention was on her at the moment. She really needed to go and put on that bra. Several things dawned on her at once. He'd changed into more comfortable clothes, he was still wearing his shoulder holster, the laptop wasn't one of hers—she had a couple of spares available at the office had she'd known he needed one—and he was wide awake.

"Yes," Ashlyn answered before veering off into the kitchen. She reached for the carafe of coffee, noticing it had been freshly brewed. Had he done that for her or was he drinking a cup? A quick glance over her shoulder showed her that he didn't have a cup near him. "Do you want some coffee? I didn't hear you leave the apartment."

"I didn't. And no, thank you," Keane responded, still studying her intently. Ashlyn turned back and concentrated on pouring herself some coffee, ignoring the fact that she'd left her other mug back in her office. "Jack brought my things up around an hour ago. Although you should know, a couple members of my team should be arriving first thing in the morning. The depth to which this perp is willing to go has altered the way your protection needs to be handled overall."

"I don't understand. What's changed?" Ashlyn asked rather cautiously, not wanting to make any additional changes in the way things were being handled. She hadn't received any emails, letters, gifts, or texts since her apartment had been cleared and her security systems upgraded. Granted, she was talking about a span of five hours, but it still felt significant to her knowing that his intrusion had been stunted. She walked back around the counter to get a better grasp on why Keane would believe reinforcements were needed. "Has something else happened?"

"No. I would have informed you if I'd received any further information." It was apparent Keane didn't appreciate that she would think he would hold back vital news, but there was no other reason for an entire team of professionals to keep an eye on her...unless he didn't want to be the one protecting her twenty-four seven. A small ache started to throb in Ashlyn's chest at the thought he harbored that much resentment toward her and she decided that maybe she didn't want to know his real motivations. "Ash, it's just a reasonable precaution."

Ashlyn's breath caught in her throat at Keane's use of the nickname he used to call her when they'd have sex. He'd said it in reference to her burning as hot as ash underneath his hands when he made love to her. He was the only man to have ever called her that and she hadn't realized just how much she'd missed the intimacy of a simple nickname. She ignored the slight, as it was apparent he hadn't even realized he'd done so when he continued to explain his reasoning.

"Coen Flynn will be renting the apartment across the hallway to monitor traffic in and out of your apartment door," Keane explained as he closed the lid to his laptop and stood. It was then she realized he was wearing jeans with a black T-shirt, instead of his preferred khakis and a pullover. "Sawyer Madison will be joining him, although he'll usually be our tail-end-Charlie. Coulter was right when he said this perp is only going to become more agitated and unpredictable. We've taken what access he had to you and completely cut it off. He'd taken the time to strategize and execute a surveillance plan and we removed it. There's no telling how he is going to react to that loss. As your hired protection detail lead, it's my responsibility to ensure we have all our bases covered."

Keane stopped close enough in front of her that she had to tilt her head up to meet his gaze. The gold flecks within his brown eyes were lighter than they usually were, reminding her of a time long ago when that had represented something entirely different. Now? He hadn't done one thing except maintain his professionalism. She reminded herself that she needed to do the same.

"I appreciate—"

The shrilling sound of the alarm system being set off cut through the stillness of the apartment, causing Ashlyn to literally jump while Keane had his weapon drawn and down by his side before her bare feet touched the ground. There was really only one access point and they were both currently looking at it. That didn't mean the intruder hadn't figured out a way in through the sealed windows, regardless that they were multiple stories off of the ground. Keane's strong grip had her turning back, motioning for her to go to her office. She would have much preferred to go to her bedroom where her Berretta was currently stowed in her nightstand, but he wasn't giving her much of a choice at the moment.

"Go," Keane barked, already moving toward the windows while maintaining an eye on the front door. "Now!"

Ashlyn backed away until she finally turned on her bare feet and ran down the short hallway, quickly making her way to her desk. She hastily reached for her desk phone, even though she knew the alarm company would have already called the authorities, only to stop mid-motion when the shrieking suddenly stopped. She listened carefully for any sign of Keane when she heard him call her name, telling her the apartment was clear. She was about to make her way out of the office when she heard her cell phone vibrate.

Call it intuition, or maybe Ashlyn was starting to think the worst of things, but she truly believed it was *him* on the other line. He'd done this. He'd triggered the alarm somehow. She wasn't sure how with all the upgrades or the fact that the FBI was most likely monitoring the system...but *he* had to be responsible for this.

Ashlyn moved some folders out of the way in search of her cell phone, finding it instantly. The display was lit with an incoming text message.

"Get your things," Keane instructed, appearing in the doorway. He abruptly stopped upon seeing her expression of fear. Ashlyn couldn't help but allow the grip of terror to take hold. This wasn't an ordinary individual. This was a determined soul bent on having her—one way or another. "Ash?"

She swallowed down the bile that had risen in her throat. With an unsteady finger, she swiped across the screen to see what he'd sent.

You should know that nothing nor no one could keep me from you.

WHY?

Why was his Ashlyn allowing others to make decisions for her? They were poisoning her against him...against their life together. All he wanted to do was shower her with the love and devotion she deserved; to see her relax after a hard day.

He needed to eliminate his enemies and get back what they had taken.

Once again, he was forced to commit a sin in the name of love. He would do so out of devotion, for she was the other half of his soul. The others had only been a pretense, a sham, to distract him from Ashlyn. He'd taught them a valuable lesson and now he had to teach others that he was to be taken seriously.

CHAPTER TEN

IT HAD TAKEN less than five minutes for Ashlyn to finally put on a bra and pack an overnight bag of clothes and toiletries, but at least a quarter of an hour to package up the files of the case she'd been working on, along with her laptop. Keane had been on his phone the entire time, coordinating with Coulter without going into specifics in case Agent West had missed a listening or audio device somewhere in Ashlyn's apartment. It would have been less than a five percent chance, but stranger things had happened and this guy had penetrated a closed security system rather quickly.

"I'll touch base when we're free and clear of this place," Keane advised over the annoying beeping sound indicating his phone was blowing up with texts and calls. No doubt Brody was trying to get ahold of him. "Meet us at zero seven hundred at the primary scheduled location."

Keane didn't have to give details of where. Coulter was well aware of Ashlyn's court docket tomorrow and her need to be at the office. Things were going to have to change, but he understood that a federal prosecutor had to go through a certain amount of hoops to get dismissed from a case...not that he'd mentioned that to Ashlyn just yet. She'd gone into a mechanical mindset and was doing what was necessary without thinking of the overall picture so far.

"Ashlyn, we need to leave. Now."

"One more thing," Ashlyn said before hurrying back to her office. Keane waited impatiently, but took the extra time provided to look at his phone. Brody had messaged that he was doing his best to follow the footprint left by the IP address that the intruder had used to breach the firewall port, but that the originating signal was now showing China. They had all flipped the switch on this guy's motor and it was only a matter of time before he crashed into a wall. It was Keane's job to make sure Ashlyn wasn't in the way when that happened. "Okay. Where are we going?"

"Somewhere safe," Keane answered vaguely, opening the door slowly and ensuring no one was out in the hallway. It was late, so it was doubtful they would run into anyone. "I'll brief you once we're underway. Jack is waiting downstairs, along with some friends of my boss. Just do as I instruct and we'll get you somewhere secure. Do me a favor, though. Don't look these guys in the eye."

Ashlyn hoisted the strap of her overnight bag on one shoulder, while carrying her briefcase and purse on the other. Keane would have immediately taken her burden, but he needed the freedom of movement to reach for his weapon or respond to a threat if needed. He carried his black duffel go-bag in one hand, having shoved everything into it that he'd need. Jack could come back and retrieve his other bag, if necessary.

"Stay to my left," Keane instructed quietly, closing the door behind them and walking down the deserted hallway. They made it to the elevator bank without a problem, but he wasn't expecting a man to appear when the sliding doors glided open. It was one of Ashlyn's neighbors, the one who'd been coming home when Keane and Coulter had been having a discussion out in the hallway. "Good evening."

"Evening," the man said with a nod, walking past the both of them without a second glance. "Excuse me."

"Go," Keane urged in a low voice, holding the doors open with his arm while Ashlyn walked into the elevator. He stepped in beside her, never turning his back while keeping his gaze fixated on the man strolling down the long hallway. Keane pressed the button for the lobby. "What's his name?"

"Jim. No, Jerry," Ashlyn corrected herself as she also stared straight ahead until the doors blocked her view. She immediately turned her attention to Keane. "He's nice. He's a veterinarian and also works at one of the emergency clinics down the street twice a week."

"Everyone's nice until you get to know them," Keane counseled, not remembering the vet's name on the list of neighbors. It was one more thing to check out and the list was growing with every passing minute. "We're heading to your office."

"What?" Ashlyn was still wearing her sweatpants, but she'd put on a pair of running shoes that had probably never been used for their actual purpose for which they had been constructed. She rarely had time to eat, let alone workout. Keane stepped in front of her as the doors to the elevator opened, revealing Jack. "Why? You're not suggesting—"

"Ma'am, let me take those for you," Jack said, interrupting what Keane knew to be an intense argument in the making. Ashlyn needed to disappear for a couple of weeks and the only way to make that happen was for her to hand over her current caseload to another federal prosecutor. "The car is right out front with the escort."

"Keane, I'm not stepping away from this case. I have an obligation to the people I'm fighting to protect," Ashlyn continued to argue, stepping in front of him to stop his progress after Jack had taken her bags. Her chestnut waves were abundant on top of her head, swinging with the momentum of her spin. Her blue eyes were wide with trepidation and she'd lost color to her already porcelain skin, but her determination not to let this man dictate how she lived her life was to be admired. It still wouldn't get him to change his mind. "Closing arguments should be in—"

"Do you want to be alive to try another case?" Keane asked, not having meant to growl the words as he had. He stepped close until they were inches apart and Ashlyn had no choice but to truly heed his warning, going so far as to bring up their past to make his point. He'd regret it later, but it was of use to him now. "Whoever this individual is, he is increasingly becoming agitated because he can't see or hear you. He has become accustomed to having you in his fantasy world. We've taken that connection from him. We have no idea what this man has done or is capable of doing to regain that contact. I stood in a courtroom five years ago and watched a man shoot your mentor in the chest and then take aim at you. I did what I had to do then. I took a man's life to change that equation, but I will never forget what it felt like to know your life could end with a couple pounds of pressure on a hair trigger. I will not stand by and watch that happen again. Do you understand what I'm saying to you?"

Keane didn't waver his stare, waiting for Ashlyn to say or do something to contradict what he was saying or diminish the terror both of them had felt that fateful day—the same day she told him he wasn't ready to be a civilian or cut out for a serious relationship. It hadn't helped that he'd asked her not an hour before to give up her dream of being a federal prosecutor and move to California to be with him. He'd called her a coward and then finally agreed that neither one of them were ready for a serious commitment. Their fate had been sealed well before a madman had entered the courtroom that day with the intent of killing the people responsible for putting his father away for murdering a federal agent.

"This isn't the same," Ashlyn whispered harshly, shaking her head and trying to reason with him. "Agent Coulter can—"

"What, Ashlyn? What can he do to keep an unknown assailant from picking any time or place to attack?" Keane asked, pushing the issue and going against his initial intuition not to physically touch her in an intimate manner. He reached up and slid his fingers behind her neck, needing her to understand the severity of the situation. "Coulter currently has no idea who is behind this and your home is no longer safe. Your life is in danger, and therefore so are the lives of others around you."

Ashlyn rested a tense fist on his chest and squeezed her eyes shut tight, the first time Keane had ever seen her so torn. She was always decisive and stood her ground, but this was a losing battle and she now understood that. He wished he'd been able to make protecting her in her own home feasible, but that just wasn't the case. He could literally hear her breathe deeply before pushing herself away from him, causing him to lower his hand.

"Fine." Ashlyn drew herself up to her five feet, six inches and wiped away the moisture that had gathered underneath her lashes. She acted as if she was about to go into court and no one was the wiser of the nerves that rattled around inside of her. The change was fascinating and commendable. "We'll go into the office and I'll get things in order to request a relief for myself on the case. The judge has the final say-so and we both know that."

Jack waited for both of them by the door, keeping a close eye on the doorman seated behind a counter positioned toward the middle of the lobby. The man was of Asian descent and watched warily as the trio walked out the door. He'd no doubt seen the somewhat heated exchange and kept his response to himself. Keane pulled Ashlyn close as they exited the building and entered the dead of night.

"Quickly," Keane urged, only releasing Ashlyn once they'd reached the town car. Jack had already opened the back door and closed her safely inside while Keane remained on the sidewalk. "Are Calvert's men in position?"

"Yes, there are a few up the street and more behind us," Jack replied, stowing the items in his hands into the trunk of the vehicle. He slammed the lid and then walked around to the driver's side, letting Keane choose which seat he'd be taking. "Everyone is in place."

Keane surveyed the somewhat busy streets filled with the night crowd. Music and laughter could be heard for blocks. There was an odor in the air that wasn't very pleasant, but the absence of humidity this time of night made it bearable. He finally caught sight of a motorcycle at the intersection, ready to lead the procession once Jack had pulled away from the curb. The rider of the Harley Davidson wasn't wearing his colors, most likely not to draw attention to the club should something happen that required gunplay.

Townes Calvert certainly hadn't run with the most respectable crowd after he'd gotten out of the service and it would be a story Keane would have to hear at some point, but the benefits of having this kind of protection far outweighed the consequences if their boy showed up with well-armed hired help. He walked around the town car and opened the back door, joining Ashlyn and inhaling the light fragrance of her lotion she'd used earlier this evening. It was much more pleasant than the stench of remnants left from the nightlife of D.C.

Keane had already disabled Ashlyn's phone by removing the SIM card and promising to get her a new one as soon as possible. She needed to go completely dark and she certainly wasn't going to like it when he instructed her to leave her laptop on her desk at the office. He wanted nothing electronic of hers to accompany them to whatever safe house Calvert was currently setting up. Her arms were crossed around her middle and she was studying his body language, most likely to see if he'd noticed anything unusual.

"We're clear, as far as I can tell," Keane assured her, reaching for his own cell phone that had been provided to him courtesy of SSI. It was a burner that had no electronic link to him and he could drop it into a trash barrel anytime he thought it was compromised. He used the speed dial that he'd setup with Brody when he got the pack of four phones from SSI's pool of burners and waited for Brody to answer. "It's me. Has Calvert found us a place to go?"

"Yes, I'll text over the details shortly," Brody said over the murmur of voices. It appeared that Calvert and someone else was in the room. "Keane, the alarm wasn't triggered remotely."

"What are you saying?" Keane asked cautiously, not liking where his friend was taking this. "Brody, I'm telling you no one was in her apartment but the two of us."

"I didn't say there was. There are sensors on the window though, and while you and I know it would be virtually impossible for someone to enter via those access points…something or someone set them off. I've tapped into the street cameras and there was nothing unusual that stood out. The window-washing scaffold was stowed and locked so it was not used. No one was directly outside any of the windows."

"You're not connecting the dots in a manner I can follow," Keane admitted, looking out the front window. The motorcycle that Keane had first noticed veered off in a different direction and another one had taken its place by the time Jack had reached the next intersection. "How was Ashlyn's alarm set off?"

"Did you, by chance, hear a low frequency rumbling of some sort?" Brody asked, searching for a response Keane was just now starting to form. Son of a bitch. "Maybe it sounded like a jet-aircraft taking off in the distance?"

"Yeah, come to think of it. A few seconds prior to the alarm going off," Keane admitted, suppressing the urge to tell Jack to turn the town car around. Whoever had managed to score the type of equipment needed to create a deep enough low frequency vibration to set off the sensors in Ashlyn's apartment wasn't playing around on his computer. He had purposefully made it so that she understood his reach. "Do you have—"

"We're currently watching the block around the apartment building, but it's most likely the parking garage across the street. He took advantage of a vulnerability inherent to the system. He's not an idiot and that makes this whole case that much more difficult," Brody explained, unable to have eyes and ears everywhere. Even those at the NSA were limited in some capacity, although their reach was far greater than his own. "The best thing for you to do is go dark until Coulter gets some type of lead on this asshole."

"We're still only contracted for protection?" Keane asked, not pleased with being so limited in his job. Ashlyn was now resting an elbow on the door, staring out the window and watching the people and buildings whiz by as Jack appeared to have hit every green light the city offered. It wasn't surprising seeing as Jack was from this area and had most likely memorized the timing of the traffic lights. "Is there a way around that?"

"No," Brody answered regrettably. "Townes called Coulter a little while ago and offered our services, but the agent currently believes he can handle the investigation as it stands. He's not a bad guy, but he's young, ambitious, and has a closing rate higher than most in his department. Taking assistance now wouldn't look so good on his résumé or in court if this ends up there."

"Then we'll need to convince Coulter that accepting support might very well enhance his career prospects," Keane recommended, never having liked politics when it came to furthering one's career. "I'll see what I can do on my end."

"You might want to be careful there," Brody counseled in a low tone, most likely to prevent Calvert from hearing him. "We're trying to build something here and it wouldn't do you any good to go dick around and screw the pooch."

"We're also protecting someone's life here," Keane stressed, not liking how his hands were tied on his end. "You and I both know that supersedes the politics of the system. We have back channels to use that the FBI can't utilize."

"Is that a compliment?" Brody asked proudly, usually not in the position to receive praise. The hierarchy of the military didn't necessarily provide commendation for off-the-books life and death procedures. Marines did their job. Period. "Don't worry. I'm working the issue quietly in the background. No one will even notice I'm there. If this guy left some clues to his identity, I'll let you know."

Keane understood that to mean Calvert had already given Brody the go-ahead to assist without really assisting. It was a fine line, but it could be done. Respect for his superior increased a little more. They covered Coen and Sawyer's presence, both of them currently on the redeye. Keane would meet up with them at the safe house. After confirming a few more things, he finally disconnected the call.

"How was my alarm set off?" Ashlyn asked, having heard every word of the conversation on his end. She definitely had patience if she'd waited this long to find out the answer. Her blue eyes zeroed in on his face, most likely catching his expression with the passing of the streetlights. "You said yourself it was just us inside my apartment."

"The person who's stalking you somehow managed to get within range of the building and use a low frequency direction transmitter to rattle one of the outside windows with just enough force to set off a vibration sensor and trigger the alarm," Keane explained, wanting to reach for her left hand currently curled into a tight fist on the fabric of her sweatpants. He didn't. It wasn't his place and he never should have touched her back in the lobby. The imaginary line they drew needed to stay in place. "He wanted you to know that he's not taking no for an answer."

"I think his text to me summed that up," Ashlyn whispered, turning her attention back out the window. She pressed her knuckles to her cheek before saying exactly what Keane was thinking. "Now we wait for him to make another move. Hopefully, he screws up at some point and reveals himself."

CHAPTER ELEVEN

A SHLYN'S EYES LITERALLY burned, as if she'd tilted her head back and purposefully poured sand into them. Her neck ached from all the stress combined with creating the motion to recuse herself from the case at this late date. It would be filed with the judge's clerk first thing in the morning.

The judge could and might still refuse her stated reason for the petition; however, that was very unlikely given the circumstances and the fact that her second chair—one of her least favorite people—had been there for all of the court appearances...save one.

Ashlyn's stomach was nauseated over what she had to do and why, and she was exhausted from the constant fear of something happening beyond her control. It did occur to her that the defendants of her case might be involved, but that was highly unlikely considering the people involved. They were pedophile flesh merchants and not too technically skilled when it came to computers. That was one of the reasons the FBI had been able to build such a solid case against them. She would have had herself a good cry if she'd thought that would do anything to relieve her situation.

The last motion was finally completed. Ashlyn sighed in resignation as she stood from her desk and started toward the office door. Keane's phone had all but been attached to his ear since they'd gotten here, but she couldn't worry about what he was setting up when she was busy disengaging from the very case she'd worked so hard on for the last six months.

That was not to mention the pile of cases she and her team had worked up for the pending court dates she might or might not be able to attend. If she was out of commission for too long, all of her caseload would be reassigned and her team would be broken up to work for other prosecutors. She might as well start all over again, having lost the confidence of the Attorney General and the U.S. Attorney's Office after failing to carry out her assigned task.

At least Ashlyn had a great team of paralegals to help her get everything filed and transferred to Bishop Vance in this last case. He wasn't her choice. The boss assigned second chairs after the court determined the docket. Bishop was the only one left standing now that the music had stopped.

Ashlyn was grateful that Mia and Parker had come into the office when she had called at two o'clock this morning to help her with the endless amounts of paperwork that had to be done in regards to such a process. It made her uncomfortable to put Mia in Bishop's crosshairs, especially since her team would be aiding him through closing arguments and awaiting reassignment. Bishop had the ability to charm a cobra, but Mia was an adult and smart enough to know when someone was blowing smoke up her skirt. As for Andrew Rutledge, he'd have to consult with one of the other federal prosecutors regarding the Haung case.

"Were you able to get ahold of Aiden or Reed?" Ashlyn asked both paralegals as she walked out of her office. She'd purposefully not called Gina in so early, knowing full well her administrative assistant would be busy fielding phone calls all day tomorrow…well, make that today. She had been briefed as to what to expect and what she would need to do once she arrived. It was going on six o'clock in the morning, but Keane had expressed his desire to leave within the next half hour, if at all possible. He was currently sitting at Gina's desk and making himself at home.

"Reed just returned our call and is heading into the office now," Parker replied, running a hand down his face as the fatigue of the night finally got to him. Reed was twenty-eight years old and had a bright future ahead of him. That was if he was able to get a handle on that girlfriend of his. She was a party girl and she tended to spend the weekends out late partying with her girlfriends to the detriment of their relationship. He was quick to learn, eager to please, and had a tendency to make the right calls at crucial moments. He was also a bulldog when it came to unearthing old case law to aid their position on current motions. "He'd accidentally turned his phone off after having it out with Cynthia again."

Ashlyn was too tired to make a cynical reply back to such a foolish and obvious sarcastic response. Reed could go far if he applied himself a little more to the work, but he still liked having the picture perfect model of a girlfriend. He was going to find that in being a responsible adult, let alone a prosecutor who was held accountable for things far beyond their control, life was a much harder won race when one tied themselves to an anchor at the start.

"And Aiden?" Ashlyn asked, handing off the last of the motions to Mia. "It's not like him to dodge my calls."

"We haven't been able to reach him, but he did say yesterday that he would be in the office by seven o'clock today," Parker informed her as he reached forward for a half-empty mug, most likely filled with bad coffee out of the office pool machine. The pool always bought the cheapest shit coffee they could find, along with generic creamer and five-pound sacks of granulated sugar. Parker's baby doll face was just an illusion, but she noticed he managed to look younger the more tired he became. "I can call you if—"

"Everything goes through Gina," Keane ordered, interrupting the conversation as he came to stand beside Ashlyn. He made eye contact with each of the duo sitting at their desks to ensure their understanding. His tone suggested no one argue with him. "No exceptions. Ashlyn's cell number won't be any good after we leave here. Gina will be given an emergency takeout number to call only in the case that one of you isn't breathing or the Attorney General dies. Ms. Ellis will return to work once the individual who's been stalking her every move is behind bars or dead."

Ashlyn bit off a few choice words, not liking the fact that she wasn't able to make her own decisions or communicate with the people she was responsible for. Well, she could have said something, but it wouldn't have been in her best interest. If she'd had her way, she'd be completing her closing arguments and carrying on with this case as if nothing was happening outside of those windows. As it was, court would probably be continued a day or two in order for Bishop to take over the case, regardless that it had come down to nearly the end. He would use her words during his closing argument.

"I need to speak with Chief Garner before we leave," Ashlyn replied, releasing her hair band and rearranging her hair so that she appeared more professional. She hadn't really been given the time to change, but she could manage some dignity by appearing composed. "Mia and Parker, is there anything else you need from me?"

"No, we'll be fine and don't worry—we have your back,"

Mia responded for both of them. She then offered up a strained smile, her worry evident in her brown eyes. "You just be safe and stay out of the line of fire."

"I'll do my best," Ashlyn replied, telling herself she really needed to walk away. Her legs wouldn't move. She couldn't do this. She couldn't just abandon a case she'd worked six months to prosecute or the life that she'd built for herself out of sheer grit and determination. There had to be some way she could—

"Ashlyn," Keane urged gently, "we need to go. Now."

She nodded and then turned on the sole of her running shoe, forcing her legs to carry her back inside her office. She reached for her father's leather satchel, instantly thinking maybe she should call her parents to give them an update on what was taking place, but she decided against it this early in the morning. She could contact them later once she was able to explain to them at length what had really happened and why she needed to get off of the grid. There wasn't anything they could do for her right now and it would only ruin their anniversary trip they'd spent a year planning.

"Ashlyn, you're going to have to leave your laptop and phone here, along with anything else that emits a signal."

She must have misunderstood Keane, because there wasn't a chance in hell she wasn't taking her only form of communication, her files, and her one remaining lifeline. He'd already removed the SIM card. Wasn't that enough?

"He hasn't touched my laptop, Keane. Only my home computer and my phone," Ashlyn said, doing her best to keep her desperation to a minimum. This was her life and it was being stripped away one piece at a time. "How am I going to—"

"We are dealing with an individual who truly believes you are an object that belongs to him. You've read all those emails and letters. The texts are stating his need to possess you while exhibiting a rather tenuous grasp of reality. You realize he's showing us he's not going to stop until he has you. I believe he doesn't care how you end up together—dead or alive. This type of psychopath will, sooner or later, flip a switch and kill someone to prove his point. He uses high-end technology to keep track of you and we have no idea how in-depth that goes…so you need to leave everything here. Your clothes will be swept for bugs before we get into the vehicle."

Ashlyn tamped down the rage that was boiling inside of her. She understood what Keane was saying, but that didn't mean she had to like it. What was she going to do with her time? Watch game shows and daytime television? She hadn't seen a soap opera since she was in middle school and stayed home sick. She didn't even watch television for anything other than the news and some occasional background noise while cooking dinner. Read? She only ever had time for law journals and case law that could aid her in court. As for something relaxing like knitting, she'd most likely end up stabbing herself with the damn needles.

She didn't have a life outside these walls.

Ashlyn slowly sank down in her desk chair and rested her forehead in the palms of her hands. She loved her chosen profession. She remembered the time her father had given her a gavel as a child and she'd sat on a sofa similar to the one in her office pretending to rule in favor of the prosecutor every time. Being an attorney had been all she'd ever wanted and now here she was left…with nothing. When was the last time she'd actually laughed at a good joke in the bar? Hell, when was the last time she'd been in a bar?

"Ashlyn—"

"Don't."

Keane had been about to give her platitudes, but she didn't need them. Not now. She also had the answer to her question and she had to wonder if she'd sequestered herself away by design. Five years ago she hadn't been this neurotic or set in her ways. She'd been spontaneous and had the best three months of her life in California, but she'd left it behind because it hadn't been in her grand plan...Keane hadn't been a part of her plan. He'd been a distraction.

Ashlyn reached for the additional files she'd kept, feeling the need for something—anything—to do while she was hidden away like a scared rabbit. That also wasn't in her nature, but it wasn't as if she had a choice. She'd rather be alive next month with another case in front of her than to be just another casualty, as Keane put it. She shoved the files, notepad, pen, and a couple of books from her bookshelf that would tide her over until she was back at work. She tried to convince herself that it wouldn't be that bad, but she failed as she finally fastened the bag.

"I'm ready," Ashlyn announced, her voice coming out a little too loud. "See? No technology."

"I spoke with Coulter a few minutes ago," Keane told her as they headed for Ashlyn's office door. Mia and Parker were nowhere in sight, most likely in the break room refilling their coffee mugs to get them through the remainder of the day. Ashlyn had spoken to Gina in general about what was taking place, but she wouldn't be in for another hour or so. She was going to need all the rest she could get to deal with the chaos, including the media. Hmmm. Ashlyn second-guessed her decision not to call her parents. She would be in dutch if they got caught unprepared. She didn't want them hearing from anyone else that she'd stepped down from such a high-profile case. Keane's voice pulled her out of going over and over all the things she should be doing instead of walking out of this office building headed to God knows where. "They are going to comb through every inch of surveillance footage they can find of your place in hopes of catching sight of someone who doesn't belong there."

"And if it's someone who actually lives in the building?" Ashlyn asked, stepping into the elevator but pressing the button for the third floor instead of the basement parking garage. She leaned her shoulder against the laminated wall, thinking she just might fall into bed and sleep the time away. The coffee she'd had earlier had long since faded from her system. "I'm to the point I'm suspecting everyone after the things Agent Coulter said."

"You mean Victor?" Keane asked as he straightened out his jacket. It was a casual blazer he'd borrowed from Jack, not wanting to enter the building with his weapon visible. It was a little tight in the shoulders, but it would do until they got back to the car. "Coulter is just doing his job. He won't eliminate anyone that could even remotely be guilty, even your friends. It's his job to find the culprit even if he has to do it based on the process of elimination."

Ashlyn mulled over what Keane had just said, another crack splitting open. Her friends were her colleagues. She worked hard to stand out. It was what she was good at. That was her life. So why, then, was she seeing just how alone she really was?

She was just tired. That was all. Agent Coulter would eventually make an arrest, Keane would go back to his new life in Florida, and Ashlyn would have her work back. She wouldn't look at their past with regret, because what made her think either one of them had changed? She obviously hadn't and he was just as determined as she was.

"Good morning, Ruth," Ashlyn said as they walked off the elevator and turned to their right, through the glass doors. Chief Garner had half of the entire third floor to himself and his staff. The other half housed the administration section—a monumental government bureaucracy that went with the United States

Attorney's Office in Washington, D.C. She wasn't surprised to see Ruth in so early, considering all the cases that had been weighing down Garner's department. "Is he in?"

"Yes, his vehicle was parked in his normal spot," Ruth replied, stepping out from behind her desk. Her fifty-year-old body was in better shape than any other woman in this building. Ashlyn half suspected Garner had picked her as his administrative assistant for that very reason. She was obsessed with Pilates and tried to convince anyone who would listen how good it was for the body. Ashlyn was envious and wouldn't be surprised if the woman outlived them all. "I was just about to go and make him a cup of coffee before disturbing his morning routine. Would you like one?"

"No, thank you," Ashlyn replied, not wanting to go into details as to why. Rumors would be flying around within the hour once Mia and Parker filed copies of the motions she'd spent all night working on and word got out that she'd transferred the Glasson case to Bishop, a relatively junior attorney. "Is it all right if I go right in?"

"Of course," Ruth granted with a smile, "you know he has an open door policy. No one ever seems to take advantage of that, though. Besides, he doesn't have an appointment until nine o'clock this morning."

And that is where Ruth became a bulldog. Everyone underneath Chief Garner was well aware of the open door policy, but they still checked with Ruth to ensure he wasn't in a meeting. She ran his schedule tighter than a gnat's ass.

"I won't be long," Ashlyn informed Keane, stepping away from the desk and knocking lightly on the door. "Chief?"

Two attorneys chose that moment to walk down the hall, their voices raised so that Ashlyn couldn't hear if Garner had called out. She knocked again and then opened the door slowly in case Ruth had been wrong about him being alone. No one was in the guest chair and music was playing softly in the background. She stepped forward when she saw Jarod at his desk, his chair turned so that she couldn't see his face.

"Chief Garner, I wanted to update you on..." Ashlyn's voice faded as something sinister began to register. There was a copper odor in the air and one she'd ever only smelled once before. No. This couldn't be happening. The room became somewhat stifling as she took another hesitant step forward, not wanting to accept what her mind was telling her. She'd left the door open behind her, but didn't want to call out to Keane for fear of looking like a scared, foolish child. She'd been up too long, that was all. Everything was fine. "Chief?"

Jarod didn't answer. Ashlyn's chest started to burn as she struggled for air and the pulsating sound of blood pounded through her ears. He was fine. He had to be. He didn't hear her come in, that was all. She took another tentative step toward the desk chair, walking slowly in an arch so she could confirm her suspicions.

Ashlyn covered her mouth in horror as she finally caught sight of Jarod's face...his lifeless eyes wide with fear and his mouth open in a silent scream that no one had heard. Blood was everywhere—soaking his shirt, down into the chair, and even pooled underneath the wheels. His throat had been slit to the point she wasn't sure how his head was still attached to his body. The arterial spray had arched across the entire bookshelf behind his desk and now the LED display of the Bose system was partially obscured by drying remnants.

Jarod Garner was dead.

In his own office.

And it was her fault.

Ashlyn jumped in fear and screamed when strong hands

grabbed her by the shoulders and spun her around.

"Ash, it's me," Keane said soothingly, pulling her into his arms. "Don't look. We need to call Coulter and we don't want to contaminate the scene any further."

Ashlyn tried to tell him what she'd found, her brain not quite processing that he was seeing the same thing. His words finally penetrated, but all that was seared into her mind was the message Garner's killer had left behind. She rested her forehead against Keane's chest as he gathered her close. Nothing could erase what she saw. The monitor on Garner's desk had been bright white, a Word document chosen to display in a large font of words no one could miss. It was burned onto the screen.

ASHLYN IS MINE

HE SMILED TENDERLY *as he watched her being escorted down the hallway, wishing he could comfort her. He longed to tell her that he was taking care of the loose threads trying to strangle their love. She would understand once she'd had time to erase that unpleasant scene from her mind.*

He hadn't expected her to be the one to find the body.

Maybe it was for the best.

It had been his gift to her, after all.

He kept his smile in place when Agent Coulter came up to ask him questions, which he was delighted to answer. Time would pass, necessary chores had to be done, and only then would he be free to go to her.

His love. His gift from God.

CHAPTER TWELVE

K EANE AND ASHLYN had arrived at a quaint two-bedroom
home located in Annapolis, Maryland by mid-afternoon.
The trip had included a vehicle change and even Keane had
dropped his burner for another in his duffle. Jack had pulled into
the garage backward and had the door closing behind them
before he'd turned off the engine. Once the few bags they had
brought were unloaded into the main house, he'd left alone via
the same way they'd arrived—quietly and gracefully.

The single story ranch was sparsely decorated with only one
overwhelming feature—the security setup was totally over the
top. The living room had a large table with several monitors
showing perimeter camera feeds and access point alarm status as
either green or red.

There were wrought iron bars covering all the windows and
doorways. An assailant would need a tank to break down one of
the three security doors with deadbolts and barricade bars
anchored into the walls and floor. Keane suspected this had
once been a drug house from the amount of security it was
utilizing. He'd seen this type of hardening before. The police had
to use armored vehicles with battering rams to gain entrance. No
one was going to slip into this house undetected.

Calvert had done well with setting Ashlyn up in a safe house within a couple hours driving distance of D.C. They'd done their best to thwart any possible way to track their progress, from changing vehicles in a specific parking garage that had no cameras to witness exchanges to using emergency vehicle U-turns while driving busy underpasses. They even included driving out of the tunnel using the maintenance access that could provide them coverage from prying overhead eyes of any type of drone camera. Keane was confident that Ashlyn's stalker had no idea where she was or any way to track her.

It needed to stay that way.

Keane had been made aware that Coen and Sawyer had landed during the time they'd still been at the office answering Special Agent Coulter's questions. They'd been setting up and securing the perimeter of the safe house at which he and Ashlyn were now staying. They had come nowhere near the U.S. Attorney's Building in D.C. Coulter came to the same conclusion as Keane—whoever had murdered Jarod Garner worked in the building and had special access.

Ashlyn knew her stalker, just as Garner had known his killer. It was someone they were used to being around and had no problem turning their back on them.

The knock that came at the door was expected, but Keane still withdrew his weapon as he verified who wanted entrance via the video feed. In addition to verifying the image on the screen, he pulled back the thin curtain on the right side sidelight of the door and made sure no was behind Coen Flynn—who matched his photo exactly—standing alone on the welcome mat dressed in a pair of jeans, a grey shirt, and a baseball cap worn backwards. Nothing flashy. Nothing very memorable in this middle class neighborhood.

Keane removed the barricade bar from its notch on the door, pulled it out of the metal insert on the floor, and stowed it in the corner. He then unlocked the deadbolt, including the lock on the doorknob, and turned the silver handle. He stepped aside without a word and waited for his new team member to enter. According to the details Brody had provided, Coen was six months straight out of the United States Marine Corps and fresh back from his third overseas tour in Afghanistan. Those intervening six months he'd worked as a private security contractor protecting high value targets from kidnapping threats.

According to his short bio, Coen had grown up in Arizona, leaving behind his parents and a younger brother who he had stayed in contact with regularly. His specialty was close combat and urban assault tactics. Most of his time in the Stan had been spent routing out insurgents who had lived in tribal enclaves in a multitude of villages surrounding Kandahar. Calvert had chosen his team well, covering all the bases while ensuring they all had done a protection detail of some sort during their tours or subsequent to their service.

"It's good to meet you," Keane said, shaking Coen's hand after securing the door behind him, including locking the bar into place with a heavy metal click. "I'm sure Calvert didn't expect you would be on this assignment so quick, but what should have been a simple case just blew up in our faces. This guy has considerable experience doing electronic surveillance."

"Brody's told me a lot about the details of the case." Coen's dark gaze slowly took in the layout of the house, only stopping when he saw Ashlyn sleeping on the couch. She hadn't stirred once in the last hour, telling Keane this was the first time she'd allowed her body to really rest. "He wanted me to let you know he's also ordered you some khaki shorts, whatever the hell that means."

Keane wasn't about to get into the fact that Brody hated his sense of fashion, saving it for another time. He motioned they should head into the kitchen, not wanting to wake Ashlyn. She needed what rest she could get.

"We've rented the apartment over the garage next door," Coen said as he leaned against the far counter, placing the bag he'd carried in next to the toaster. He adjusted his cap, lifting it enough to show the length of his black hair. It was long enough to signify he hadn't cut it for a few months. "Sawyer is setting up the equipment and we have a clear view of the front, along with the approach up and down the street in either direction. We'll have to make perimeter checks of the backyard, seeing as the proximity of the surrounding houses and the construction being very similar tends to obscure our view of the backside of the property. The number of privacy fences in the neighbors' backyards have created dead zones that prevent us from a clear assessment, except when directly patrolling those areas. So stay clear of the backyard as a general rule."

"Has Coulter approved SSI's involvement in the investigation?" Keane asked, already knowing the answer. Brody had been in close contact with him, but things could change on a dime. "Stalking a federal prosecutor and hacking into her personal network is one thing. The murder of Chief Jarod Garner? This puts the case into a whole other ballgame and the press coverage is now in full force. The feds are going to need all the help they can get."

"Which is why Coulter's superiors are maintaining centralized control of the case. To be quite honest, we'd have to be idiots to want to participate in investigating at this point. They'll be looking to find someone to blame for the Bureau's failures thus far. An independent firm might just suit their purposes," Coen warned, resting the palms of his hands on the counter behind him. "This is going to turn into a nationwide manhunt because of the bloodshed this guy has left behind. The media isn't going to let this go and Ashlyn Ellis' life is going to be dissected on the six o'clock news for all to see. We follow protocol, keep the primary safe, and wait this out. The perpetrator will screw himself up somehow, sooner or later."

Keane didn't reply right away, quelling his instinct to do something other than sit around. He hadn't realized the transition of occupations would be this much of a struggle. Ashlyn had thought it was perfectly okay for her to walk into an office he'd yet to clear for her security, but she'd opened the door before he could stop her. He'd followed close behind and had recognized the sour odor of death right away, as had she.

The look on Ashlyn's face would stay with him forever…the disbelief, the horror, the disgust, and the self-incrimination. He'd still yet to talk to her in-depth about what had happened back at the office. The majority of the morning had been spent going over statements with Coulter and then allowing Ashlyn to speak with Bishop Vance regarding the transfer of the Glasson case.

Every single person in the U.S. Attorney's Building was shaken by what had occurred and Ruth had needed medical assistance when she'd gone into a full-blown panic attack, having missed any clues of the murder of her boss. Pilates could only get you so far.

"I figure you might want something to do in your spare time, though," Coen said, pulling out papers that had been folded vertically so they would fit into his back pocket. He tossed them just right, so that the bulk of the thickness hit the kitchen table. Keane pulled out a chair and took a seat, reaching for whatever gift Coen was offering. "That's the list of names of those who were in and out of the building during the elapsed time since Garner had arrived and the discovery of his body. Apparently, the feds have video footage of him arriving in the underground parking garage around zero four hundred. Not even his assistant could give a reason why he would have been at the office at that time."

"Where did you get this?" Keane asked, looking over the catalog of names. The building was large and thus a rather high count of employees. Several names were highlighted and he recognized the reason why.

"Let's say I have a friend in the Bureau who owes me a favor or two," Coen replied, not revealing his sources. Brody had mentioned that Coen had quite a few contacts in the city and Keane was starting to realize just how far those contacts went up the ladder. "Victor Wright is currently Coulter's prime suspect. He's being questioned and has already retained a lawyer, although claiming his innocence the whole way."

"I can see why they would automatically make that assessment, but how did Wright gain access to Ashlyn's apartment?" Keane continued to go down the list of names, recognizing that Aiden Younger was included. That couldn't be right. He looked up to find Coen staring at the arched entryway from the living room. "Ashlyn, we didn't mean to wake you."

"That's okay," Ashlyn replied, looking a little worse for wear. She was in the same clothes as last night, her hair still pulled back at the nape of her neck, and she had absolutely no color in those high cheekbones of hers. She was still downright beautiful and Keane had never met another woman who could come close to compare. Her blue eyes were shifting between the paper in his hand and Coen. "And you are?"

Keane rose from the table and caught the raised eyebrow Coen had given in response to Ashlyn's inquiry. She was standing tall and doing her best to maintain the professional manner perfected over time and many accomplishments. She had a heart of gold and an attitude of steel. It was an intriguing combination that had caught his attention five years ago and still had the ability to amaze him today.

"Coen Flynn—recent acquisition of SSI," Coen said, introducing himself while stepping forward with an extended arm. "I'm part of your perimeter security team, as well as a hulk by the name of Sawyer Madison. We're here should anything or anyone attempt to put your life in danger or spoil your solitude."

Ashlyn's life *was* in danger, but those employees of SSI could mitigate the degree. She reached out and shook Coen's hand, a tentative smile replacing the stern expression she'd walked into the kitchen with.

"You were talking about Victor," Ashlyn pointed out, reaching for the paper in Keane's hand. He relinquished it, not willing to keep her in the dark. She had every right to know who would have had an opportunity to kill Jarod Garner. "He didn't do this. He doesn't have it in him. He didn't stalk me and he certainly didn't commit murder."

Ashlyn read through the names as she slowly turned and walked back into the living room. Both Keane and Coen followed her, hoping she would see something that would give Coulter a leg up. It was doubtful, but anything was possible. She reached into the leather case she'd brought with her and pulled out her pen, immediately sitting down on the couch and crossing off names. Having a purpose had given Ashlyn some color back.

"The people I'm crossing off the list are females," Ashlyn explained, glancing up for confirmation. "Didn't Agent Coulter say the profile he was using was of a white male in his thirties? We should be able to narrow the list down to a handful of men whom fit that description. As for Victor, he's in his forties and I'm sure there is no proof he was in my apartment building last night."

"Profiles are loosely based on the facts provided in that case," Keane warned, not wanting Ashlyn to get ahead of herself. She understood quite well how profiling worked, but she didn't want to heed her own advice. "He could be a she that sees herself as a dominant in a relationship. Ages can be off by a few years in either direction based on maturity and not physical age…but the one thing that can't change is this individual's knowledge in everything and anything to do with technology. You understand why Coulter would single out Victor."

"Then why not Paul?" Ashlyn offered up another scapegoat in her attempt at convincing herself Victor could not be the culprit. She tapped her pen to the paper. "There's also Ben, Craig, and Ryan who are in the same department with the same extensive skillset. They were all there at that hour, most likely working on the Haung case."

"I'm sure Agent Coulter will contact Townes Calvert, per our protocol, and give us updates on the interrogations he's conducting," Coen said in order to appease Ashlyn's doubts, setting down the black duffel bag he'd grabbed off the kitchen counter. "In the meantime, I brought a couple weapons, ammo, and a few additional pieces of security surveillance equipment I'd like to set up at the back of the property."

Keane reached for the Px4 Storm chambered in .40 caliber Smith & Wesson, weighing the firearm in his hand. It was similar to the 92 FS model Berretta she kept in her room, with a bit more punch, and would make her at ease should she need to use it. Coen also handed him a Sig Sauer P220 Elite, for which Keane would use as a backup. He took the four extra magazines of 230 grain hydra-shock rounds as well.

Ashlyn had been staring at Coen with curiosity and Keane admitted to a stab of jealously, even though he wasn't remotely entitled to such an emotion when it came to her. It wasn't until she spoke up that she unknowingly alleviated the uncomfortable position he found himself in.

So much had happened within the last thirty-six hours that Keane hadn't had time to dwell on them or their past. It was always simmering underneath the surface, from when he would catch Ashlyn studying him, when they touched innocently, or when either one of them brought up the past. He'd known the moment he'd set eyes on her that they had never truly finished what they'd started five years ago.

"I know you from somewhere," Ashlyn exclaimed in a strange, somewhat crazy kind of puzzlement. The arched brows above her blue eyes came down as she struggled to recall where to place Coen's face. Keane looked between the two, curious now as to where she would have known Flynn, especially considering that he'd just come back from a personal security contract in Mexico City. "Your brother—"

"Is home in Arizona and staying out of trouble now," Coen replied with a hardened tone, picking up the black duffel bag with a small degree of agitation. He adjusted his ball cap once more, this time so the bill faced the front and shadowed his face. "If you'll excuse me, I'm going to head out back and set up this gear while the neighbors are still at work."

Keane didn't know his new team members that well, but everyone had the right to their own privacy. He had nothing to hide, but he sure as hell didn't want his personal business to be fodder for the gossip mill once they all got back to Florida. Whatever had happened to Coen's brother was enough to cause him some measure of discomfort and could only lead to dissention among the small group of operators. That's the last thing they needed to happen between the team members on this case.

"I didn't mean to upset him," Ashlyn said as she watched Coen disappear from view. Her vexed blue eyes returned to Keane. "You don't know?"

"I don't want to know," Keane corrected her before taking the piece of paper out of her hand. "I don't know Coen all that well, but men in general don't want their family secrets to follow them wherever they go. This job might be Coen's way to wipe the slate clean. Regardless, Calvert has vouched for him and that is all I need to know to place my life in his hands."

Ashlyn nodded her agreement and then shook her head slightly as if to clear it from any disruptions or further distractions. She still appeared exhausted, but her mind was evidently spinning enough that she wouldn't be able to close her eyes for a while.

"Why don't we get some coffee and then go over this list in detail?" Keane suggested, holding out his hand for her to take. He wasn't sure what prompted him to do so, but he was finding it very hard not to cross that line that separated professionalism from becoming too personal with Ashlyn. "Maybe we can find something to help Special Agent Coulter since you're so sure Victor isn't behind this mess."

"He's not, of that I'm sure," Ashlyn said with resolve, slipping her delicate hand into his. She was a mass of contradictions, because he believed beyond a shadow of a doubt that she could do what was needed to survive if that time ever came. She was strong, intelligent, and cunning in a way that was admirable. "But after looking at that list...I think I might know who it is, after all."

CHAPTER THIRTEEN

A SHLYN LAY IN bed and listened to the silence as the wheels in her head spun. She'd thought maybe she had all of this figured out, but Keane had said Paul Bostle couldn't be the one who had murdered Jarod Garner. Even though the IT technician's name was on the list and he had the required skillset, he'd apparently been in with Bishop Vance during the time in question. Bishop had somehow gotten a Trojan virus from searching the Internet on his desktop at work, which had set him back for his upcoming day in court on some random national monument trespass case brought about by some group's nonviolent protest, advocating free college tuition for certain special interest groups. It also would have postponed the Glasson case, but she couldn't think about that now. That ruled out Paul and Bishop.

She wondered if she was a horrible person to think that someone she'd worked with for a couple of years could actually be a murderer. Paul had been nothing but nice to her and more than a bit helpful ever since she'd met him. Yes, he was a little odd socially. But that certainly didn't make him a stalker and now a killer. Is this what she had been resorted to, suspecting someone because they knew how to use a computer better than her? Dissecting other people's personalities and labeling them something they weren't because she didn't understand their motives?

Ashlyn turned on her side, the roughness of the sheets letting her know they were new and hadn't been broken in yet. They needed to be run through the dryer with a few dryer sheets. Maybe that would be a small contribution she could make tomorrow while they passed the day. She pulled the other pillow close to her chest and willed herself to close her eyes. Instead, she found herself staring at the open door. Keane had asked that she keep it open and she had, although she would have felt safer in the same room with him. That would only be asking for trouble.

Dennis Paavo or Adam Walker. Ashlyn turned to face the wall, the light blue appearing darker than when it was daylight. Both men had been in the elevator with her the other day. She'd turned Dennis' invitation to dinner down a couple of times. She just didn't have the time or desire to date anyone, especially a coworker. She'd told Agent Coulter that, but nothing had ever come of it. He hadn't been in the building last night, though. Had Adam? She didn't recall seeing his name on the list.

Keane had told Coen to contact Agent Coulter to let him know Aiden's name had shown up on the list, but yet he hadn't been in the office that morning with them. Had someone used his credentials? Ashlyn refused to believe that Aiden could be responsible for all of this, considering the man spent what time off he did have at an animal shelter or at his local community center fostering his Animals for Elders program. No one who loved animals as much as he did could have sliced a man's throat down to the—

Thud.

Ashlyn sat straight up, looking around the room. She instinctively held her breath, listening for where the noise had come from. Her skin prickled at the thought of being found, but wouldn't Coen have seen someone lurking around the house? What if he and his partner had fallen asleep across the street in their garage apartment? What if whoever was supposed to be watching the house had needed to go to the bathroom for just a second? Or get something to drink out of the refrigerator?

Thud.

"Shit," Ashlyn whispered frantically, reaching for the Px4 Storm on the nightstand. She inhaled somewhat evenly now that she had a powerful firearm in the palm of her hand, giving herself the ability to protect herself. No one could hurt her inside these walls...not with the amount of security this house provided. But had Keane heard the same noise? It appeared to be coming from outside, but she couldn't be sure.

Ashlyn didn't want to turn on the bedroom light for fear of letting whoever was out there know she'd heard them coming. She hadn't felt comfortable changing into something that would make her feel vulnerable, so she'd kept on the sweatpants and a T-shirt, minus the running shoes. She was grateful for that as she set the bottom of her feet onto the cold hardwood floor. The bed squeaked as she stood from the mattress, causing her to wince in fear of someone hearing the uncoiling of the springs.

Ashlyn took a tentative step forward, listening as closely as she could to the air around her. Nothing. It was silent once again. She still held her weapon out in front of her, trained on the doorway. Her finger was aligned with the barrel and not the trigger, the way she'd been taught. She flicked the safety off to make the weapon condition one—ready to fire. She wouldn't shoot unless absolutely necessary, and even then...she would ensure her target's identity before firing at anyone.

"Ashlyn."

"Jesus Christ!" Ashlyn whispered harshly as she turned the

corner of the small hallway. Keane was standing there with his firearm in hand, wearing nothing but a pair of khakis. He'd taken a shower earlier when Coen was still here, but his hair was still damp. "You're lucky I didn't shoot you."

"Which is why I said something before you rounded the corner and realized I was here." Keane kept his tone low as he moved forward. Ashlyn lowered her weapon and took a step back when he advanced, placing a warm hand on her arm. The difference in temperature was obvious from the way his fingers practically burned her flesh. "I want you to go into the bathroom, lock the door, and stay there. You don't come out for anyone but me. Do you understand?"

"Yes, but you can't go out there your—"

"Ashlyn, my job it to protect you, not the other way around," Keane explained all the while guiding her to the small bathroom at the end of the hall. He flipped the light switch, although used the dimmer so the light wasn't that bright. "Remember, do not open this door for anyone but me."

Ashlyn would have argued had Keane not shut the door behind him. She was surprised to see a deadbolt installed and she went ahead and fastened it, not appreciating being put in a box. She understood the reasoning, but wouldn't they have benefited with both of them out there to watch each other's back? Now, Keane was on his own until he got in touch with Coen and Sawyer…and that might be too late if the bad guy was out there.

She leaned against the door, resting her ear on the painted wood. Was Keane still there? Or had he already walked down the hallway? Was he going to go outside? Ashlyn didn't like being kept in the dark. How was she supposed to make the right decisions when she didn't have all of the information? What if Coen came to the door and told her it was all right to come out? Should she open the door?

Questions and more questions, doubt after more doubt plagued her as she waited for any sign that Keane had been hurt. He'd said he was doing his job, but he wasn't just her protector. He was more and that was something they both needed to address. Would they be given the opportunity? What if he was hurt tonight? What if he died like Jarod? What if—

"Ash, come on out," Keane called from somewhere in the house. Ashlyn closed her eyes in relief and rested her head against the thick wood. She couldn't continue to go on like this. She wasn't acting like herself and she was allowing this…criminal…to have power over her. It was time to stop being afraid. "Ash?"

Ashlyn flipped the deadbolt and opened the door, figuring Keane was close from the sound of his voice. He stood there studying her with concern, but she was okay. She really was. She didn't give him a chance to react, other than bring his arms around her when she walked right up to him and pressed her body against his.

Neither said a word as they held each other. Keane's arms wrapped tighter around her waist. It felt so good…so right…to be in his arms. She wasn't sure how long they stayed together, standing in the hallway embracing each other, but it was Coen's voice that had them separating. She hadn't realized she'd been standing on her tiptoes until she lowered herself to the ground and looked up at Keane.

"You're safe, Ash," Keane murmured, using a finger to tuck the loose strands of hair back behind her ear. His brown eyes searched hers for answers she didn't have. She only wanted to remain in his arms a while longer. "It was just a raccoon. He was trying to tip the neighbor's garbage can over."

"It's clear," Coen called out from somewhere in the living room. Keane leaned forward and tenderly pressed his warm lips to her forehead before taking her by the hand and walking her down the hallway. Sure enough, Coen was standing by the door. He didn't say a word or even acknowledge the fact that Keane held her hand. "I'm heading back. Sawyer doesn't like it when I leave him for too long. He gets lonely."

"That needy, is he?" Keane fired back, finally letting go of Ashlyn's hand to reach for his shirt. "I'll have to remember that."

"Shit," Coen expressed with wit as he adjusted his ball cap. "I'm learning quite a lot about my new teammates. You knew Brody back in the day. Were you aware that Brody's sister is Camryn Novak, the actress from that sci-fi movie? Sawyer's in love."

Ashlyn glanced at Keane, who had just drawn a short-sleeved, navy blue shirt over his head. He was smiling as if the last fifteen minutes hadn't happened. Her heart still hadn't settled from the terror that the individual who killed Jarod Garner—in cold blood—had found her. This was no longer a harmless voyeur looking through a camera lens at her or a distant stalker looking for his prey, but a killer seeking to eliminate those who were protecting her so that he could claim his prize.

"You tell Sawyer that Brody might seem like a surfer boy who's more concerned with the height of the waves rolling in than a protective older brother, but trust me when I say I've seen Brody in action when it counts. He might like his high-end tech gizmos, but he can use a knife better than anyone I know and come out the other end a winner."

"Oh, man," Coen said with a laugh, his fingers covering the door handle. "I can't wait to get back to Florida to see how this goes over. You two guys try and get some rest. From what Brody just relayed to us…it appears an arrest might be made by tomorrow."

"Victor?" Ashlyn asked, looking to Keane for any kind of confirmation. She didn't want to believe it was true. "Did he confess?"

"No, not yet," Keane replied, walking across the room so he could lock up behind Coen. He pulled back the curtain just enough for him to look outside. "Coulter somehow believes Victor is the person responsible though. Let's face it, he certainly has the experience needed to do what was done to your security system and home computer network."

"Then why wouldn't Victor have used the new system he had Noah install instead of being somewhere outside the building with low frequency transmitter equipment to rattle the windows? Can Coulter even prove Victor was outside my apartment building at the time it happened?" Ashlyn wasn't connecting the dots because none of this was making sense. "What if I talk to—"

"No," Keane replied, instantly shutting down Ashlyn's attempt at resolving some unanswered questions. He gestured toward her weapon. "You should really put your firearm on safe and put it back into your holster. You're protected here."

"Not from raccoons, apparently," Ashlyn offered up with a half-smile, wishing her unease didn't just stem from someone stalking her or killing her friends. Jarod and she hadn't been what she considered close, but she had thought of him as a friend. She realized Keane was right. "We're in a safe house in the middle of Annapolis, Maryland with two SSI agents across the street monitoring my safety. I brought zero technology with me and I mentally know you're right…there is no possible way for this man to know where I am. Besides, who would think to look inside a bright green house with yellow shutters? But what about those still back home? What has come of Mia, Parker,

Aiden, and Reed? Mia and Parker were in the office with me while Jarod was being murdered. Reed wasn't even in the building. I know Aiden's card key was used to enter the garage entrance, but trust me when I say he couldn't have killed Jarod. Agent Coulter will figure out what happened with Aiden, but in the meantime…are any of them truly safe?"

Ashlyn wasn't about to return to an empty bedroom with uncomfortable sheets where she would toss and turn until morning. She sighed and made her way into the kitchen instead. She remembered seeing a teakettle on the stove. Maybe that would help ease her anxiety.

"I'm sure Agent Coulter has spoken to everyone who's…"

"Close to me?" Ashlyn asked, placing her weapon on the counter. She reached for the kettle and then filled it with water. She turned around to watch Keane's reaction. Was he telling her everything? "Gina? My team? Anyone who might have had a hand in bringing the FBI in? That was me, Keane. Only me. This…man…has turned into a cold-blooded killer because—"

"No, it wasn't only you," Keane informed her with caution, pulling a chair out from the kitchen table and taking a seat. He started composing a text message. "Jarod Garner is the one who called in SSI to protect you."

"But no one knew that." Ashlyn recalled Agent Coulter saying that her office had been cleared from any listening or audio devices. No one had known it was Jarod's doing to bring in the services of a security firm with the exception of—

"Victor knew," Keane answered for her, glancing up with concern. She wasn't ready to accept a scapegoat as an answer, so she concentrated on turning on the burner and set the kettle on top of the stove. "No wonder Coulter feels comfortable with his chosen suspect."

"It can't be Victor. He isn't that kind of person," Ashlyn

protested once again, still unable to bring herself into believing that the mild-mannered man could be responsible for such a grisly murder. She leaned against the counter and crossed her arms, willing the cold away that had settled into her bones. "I still think the FBI are all wrong on this one. It's someone else."

"Either way, we're safe miles away from the city," Keane reassured her. He'd sent his message and looked just as comfortable now as he did when Ashlyn would return to her hotel room after being in court each day all those years ago. It was wrong on so many levels for her to stand here at a time like this, recalling what he'd looked like without that shirt over his chest. She lifted a hand and pressed her thumb and finger against her eyes to wipe away the image. "I know it's difficult for you to sit on the sidelines while someone else is in the thick of things, but this is hard for me too."

"Because you want to be out there catching a killer or because you're stuck here with me?" Ashlyn hadn't meant to say that, but the words had flown out of her mouth before she could bite her tongue. "I'm sorry. There's just a lot of unresolved…"

"Yes, there is." Keane hadn't moved from his place in the chair. Why, then, had the tone of his voice become more intimate? Ashlyn lowered her hand and admonished herself for being a coward. It wasn't in her nature, so she met his heated gaze. Her heart accelerated at the implication of what he was telling her. "We haven't had time to address the issue of *us*. I'm honestly not sure we should, because little has changed with the exception that I'm at a point in my life where I'm ready for more. I do know that I want you with just as much desire and validity as the day I met you walking into that courtroom."

Ashlyn couldn't prevent the memories from their time together from crashing over her like a tidal wave. She'd been working a case that had crossed multiple state lines, ending in

California where the trial had taken place. The last thing she'd expected was to have an attraction to one of the LAPD SWAT members who'd come to testify against the last defendant standing.

One invitation for drinks had turned into a three-month long love affair, both of them agreeing it was a temporary fling that burned with the intensity of a lightning strike. Except they hadn't stuck by the rules, had they? Every night Keane would show up at her hotel door until she'd finally given him his own key card and he would stay all night. She'd quickly gotten used to his presence, comforted by his voice, and addicted to his unique touch. Yet there had always been a side to him that was uncontrollable, a part of him that was just beyond her reach. He might have physically left behind the military, but his mental being had remained elusive. He craved the adrenaline only those combat tours had provided him and she hadn't been enough to satisfy his needs.

"The things I said that day were…"

"The truth?" Keane asked, admitting in his own way she'd been right. He quietly set his phone on the table. "I wanted you. That was the truth. Was I ready to give up what was keeping me from going stir crazy? Was I ready to move to a different coast from where my family could drive down to see me on the weekends? Was I ready for any kind of marriage? No. And neither were you, at the time. I recall saying some mighty cruel words back in your direction, but we are both very passionate people who stand by our beliefs and our convictions."

"Why now?" Ashlyn asked, needing to know what was different. He claimed he was, but what about her? She hadn't realized just how lonely her life had become until now, when she'd had to hand over a list of friends. She'd sequestered herself away from everyone of consequence, just like those jurors when she suspected that they might be distracted when she asked them to make a life and death decision. Was that the way to live for any amount of time? Was that the kind of life she wanted for her future? She'd thought it was, but Keane had given up the one thing that had prevented him from having more. The possibilities were endless for him. "Why give up your career and move to another coast, away from your family?"

Ashlyn hadn't realized just how still Keane had been until he leaned forward, startling her with his movements. She swore the heat of his gaze was going to consume her and it was as if the rest of the world and its problems faded away. The irresistible passion she'd come to crave was showing itself once again and she braced herself for the inevitable. She'd survived the conclusion once before, but she wasn't so sure she had what it took to endure another tryst without giving up a part of herself...her heart was vulnerable.

"I was tired. So, so tired," Keane admitted honestly with a shake of his head, spreading his hands in a helpless manner. He was anything but powerless, proving that with the life-altering decision he'd made recently. "I wanted a quieter life—one where I can still make a difference in people's lives while finally having one of my own. I will always feel the pull, Ash. It's continually there and it's powerful, but I finally found a peace within myself after taking a fishing trip with my father. He hardly ever spoke of his time in Vietnam, but he finally shared with me what it was like and how he dealt with life after the war. It wasn't easy for him. It's never easy, no matter what kind of battle or war we face. We all change inside. The men and women who sacrifice a part of themselves for their country do not come back the same person as when they left. Returning home was the beginning of a healing process and something I needed to work out on my own. We met at a time when I was still adjusting to civilian life. Call it the wrong time or the wrong place, but fate eventually played out and now we find ourselves at another crossroads further down each other's road."

Ashlyn listened closely to every word Keane said, taking every one of them to heart. He didn't blame her for the things she'd said, just as she didn't fault him. The weight of shouldering culpability lifted slightly, but it wasn't completely gone. It wouldn't be erased until one of them decided to sever this passionate connection that had already grown roots.

Ashlyn wasn't sure what she wanted anymore or if they even had the ability to claim what they once had, but she knew without a doubt that she didn't want the cold existence she found herself living. Every time Keane touched her or held her, she found herself craving his heat like nothing else. No other man had ever warmed her soul the way he had and she didn't want to lose that all over again without being honest with each other. Keane would go back to Florida when this was all said and done without so much as a cruel word if that's what she wanted. She didn't.

Fate had provided them another opportunity and Ashlyn truly believed this would be the only one given to them. Neither of them could see into the future of how this would all pan out, because it was up to them to make the decisions of how the rest of their lives were to proceed.

She wanted this. She wanted him. She wanted more than what she had.

"This crossroads you speak of," Ashlyn said softly while taking a step forward, having already made up her mind. She had no idea where this path would lead them, but they deserved to see it through, given that they'd just witnessed how quickly mortality could be taken from them. Keane leaned back so he could look up at Ashlyn as she stopped directly in front of him.

His brown eyes studied her with an intensity that stole her breath. "Which direction would you like to go?"

"Any route except the one that would lead us back to where we ended up." Keane lifted his hand until he was able to intertwine his fingers with hers. He pulled her closer in between his legs so that she had to rest her other palm on his shoulder. Her heart raced as she comprehended the weight of the choice they had just made. Things would never be the same after tonight for either of them. "I don't know what the future holds for us, but I'd like to find out, if you would do me the honor."

Ashlyn never abandoned their connection as she drifted her fingers up his neck and cradled his jawline. The intimacy from such a simple act was overpowering. Her mind, body, and soul came alive as if they'd all been asleep for these five long years. Maybe they had been. She didn't know for sure and she no longer wanted to dwell on it.

"I'd like to find out, too," Ashlyn whispered, leaning down and brushing her lips softly across his. She lifted her lashes to see the gold flecks of his eyes shimmering with arousal. "Make love to me, Keane."

HE POUNDED HIS *fist against his forehead, wanting to erase the sordid images of what was taking place. He'd killed for her. He'd taken a life so they could have one of their own…together.*

This is how she repaid him?

The FBI had no idea how far his reach went or the fact that he now knew exactly where Keane Sanderson had taken Ashlyn. Agent Coulter was too busy with his prime suspect to notice anything else, so he was free and clear to do as he pleased to whom he pleased.

What would please him more than Keane Sanderson's blood?

He wanted to hurt Ashlyn the way she'd hurt him. She was no longer the woman he thought she was—no longer innocent.

She now needed to join the others who had disappointed him.

She didn't know it yet, but he was coming for her and she would suffer as he had suffered.

CHAPTER FOURTEEN

"**T**HERE'S NO WALKING away when this case is over," Keane warned her as he slowly stood and cradled her face in the palms of his hands. He drank in Ashlyn's beauty, nothing as trivial as makeup inhibiting his view. Her long chestnut hair hung down her back in unrestrained waves as she tilted her head back and studied him with those stunning blue eyes of hers. He needed her to understand that they weren't agreeing to anything that was casual like before. This was a different time and a different place. "We see where this leads, from beginning to end."

"Agreed," Ashlyn whispered, running her fingers through his hair and bringing him closer to her. Keane didn't object in the least. "Now stop wasting time and take me."

Keane smiled and instantly hoisted Ashlyn up so that her legs wrapped around his waist. He wanted nothing more than to take her to bed, but he needed to ensure her safety as well. That was paramount. He kissed her passionately as he walked over to where her weapon lay on the counter. Together, they took care of business without stopping what they were doing. She grabbed her firearm while he shut off the burner on the stove, preventing the kettle from whistling. He'd also put his cell phone in his back pocket in case Coen or Sawyer needed to get ahold of him.

It wasn't long before Keane walked them toward the bedroom where Ashlyn had done nothing but toss and turn the first half of the night. He'd heard every sound the mattress made as she tried to get comfortable. Those two words—toss and turn—took on a new meaning as he stopped by the side of the bed and slowly lowered her feet to the ground. The rest of the night would pass by with much more pleasure, and hopefully by morning they would have an answer with Victor's pending arrest.

Keane pushed away all thoughts regarding what was taking place in D.C. As it had been pointed out several times, he was only responsible for Ashlyn's personal protection. She was safe and sound in his arms and he intended to keep her that way for the next several hours at the very least.

Ashlyn had never turned on the lamp positioned on the nightstand, which meant only thin beams of moonlight illuminated the room. It was more than enough to drink in her beauty. Keane gently took the weapon from her hand and set it down by the alarm clock, within easy reach. It was as if he'd pulled the trigger on their passion. Each of them slowly undressed in front of each other, eager for another taste of one another while still taking their time to enjoy the view.

Keane took off his shoulder holster, setting both the leather case and his weapon on the floor in case it was needed. The one thing they couldn't do without was the condom currently in his wallet. He made sure it was on the bedside table, as well. Within a matter of minutes, both of them stood vulnerable in front of each other. The thing of it was, he didn't consider himself defenseless with her. He felt invincible.

Ashlyn stood at five feet, six inches in her bare feet. Her breasts were more than a handful and Keane appreciated their sensitivity. He reached out now and brushed a thumb across her nipple, feeling it harden underneath his touch. He heard her quick inhalation and he swore that sharp sound traveled through his body. There was nothing more satisfying than pleasing a woman, although not just any woman.

"Your response to my touch is as breathtaking as it ever was," Keane murmured, taking his hand and trailing his fingers down the curved side of her breast. He didn't stop as he traced the valley of her waist and over her hip. Her arms had been by her sides, but it seemed she didn't want to waste time. Her warm hands rested on his chest as she took a step forward. "I never did get my fill of you and I highly doubt I ever will. You're like an addiction I can't shake."

Ashlyn took matters into her own hands and pushed away from him, lying back against the tousled sheets and reaching out her arms. He didn't hesitate to slip in between her legs, resting himself against her. He propped himself up on his elbow to give him leverage and leaned in to press his lips softly against her neck. She'd tilted her head to give him more access and he inhaled the fragrance of the shower gel she'd used earlier. It wasn't what she normally used, but it was still *her* all the same. She was downright intoxicating.

"I missed you," Keane whispered honestly, pulling back enough so that he could watch Ashlyn's reaction. She had never truly allowed him inside of her life, but there didn't appear to be any barriers between them this time. "I never realized how much until this very moment."

Keane didn't give Ashlyn time to respond. He began to love her the way she deserved. Every touch, stroke, and caress was meant to convey his feelings. There wasn't a place on her body that he didn't pay attention to in some way or another. By the time he was done, he'd left them both wanting only more.

Ashlyn turned them so that Keane was resting on the bed

and she was straddling him. Her hair hung over her shoulder, covering and moving lightly across his chest and she, too, had her way with him. She returned the affection and by the time they each had their turn...they were both breathless and in need of more.

"Here," Ashlyn whispered, sitting up and reaching behind her for the condom he'd set on the nightstand. "Let me have this pleasure."

"Your touch is all the indulgence I need," Keane countered, telling her nothing but the truth. "You take what you need from me, Ashlyn."

Ashlyn's smile was bright enough to see even in the semi-darkness. They were both shaking with need, most likely having taken too long to reach this point. She was right, though. They had each acquired their own pleasures, but yet there was so much more to be had.

Keane watched closely as Ashlyn tore the foiled package and removed the lubricated disc. She took her time fitting the latex over him, prolonging the exquisite torture he was experiencing underneath her fingertips. She lifted herself and positioned his tip at her entrance.

They both closed their eyes as instinct took over. Ashlyn rested her hands on his chest, using him as leverage as she rotated her hips around and down. By the time she started to lift herself off of her knees, Keane only had to rest his hands lightly on her waist as she controlled her movements, taking both of them to the highest heights of pleasure.

They had spent the rest of the night hours getting reacquainted and taking small breaks in between. They had to improvise since they'd only had access to one condom, but there were other ways to pleasure one another. Morning light was streaming through the shades by the time they were done. Keane pulled Ashlyn close and held her tight, knowing fate had already decided their future. They just needed to stop and listen long enough to get it right this time. It wasn't every day that people were given a second chance, let alone for those in his chosen profession.

Keane heard the vibration of his cell phone before it woke Ashlyn, so he answered quickly, knowing she needed her rest. He wasn't so sure she would get the sleep she needed after he'd answered the call.

"Aiden Younger was found dead in his apartment," Townes Calvert informed him from only one place that could have the incessant whirling sounds in the background. "I'm headed to D.C. myself by the request of the Attorney General. Victor Wright isn't who we are looking for. He has an airtight alibi for the time of death and has been nothing but cooperative. We're looking for someone else, Sanderson. Ms. Ellis isn't safe to return to the city until an actual arrest has been made. See to it that no harm comes to her."

Keane had pushed himself up on his elbow to take the call, but it had also given him leverage to watch Ashlyn sleep. He didn't want to tell her that one of her paralegals had been another casualty by the hands of this monster who was after her. He didn't want to tell her they were no closer to catching the son of a bitch than they had been before.

"Don't worry, Calvert," Keane answered in a soft tone so as not to disturb Ashlyn. Her light brown lashes were resting against her flushed cheeks, the first time he'd seen color in them since he'd reentered her life. "I'll keep Ashlyn safe, no matter the cost."

CHAPTER FIFTEEN

A SHLYN WIPED AWAY another tear with the endless stream of tissues Keane had given her, blowing at some strands of hair that were sticking to the side of her face. She ended up moving them out of the way with trembling fingers. All that did was make her mad, because she absolutely hated the fact that she was being made to feel so helpless by this cowardly piece of shit. It had taken most of the morning to digest what had happened to her small world of coworkers, but not being able to be with Gina, Mia, Parker, and Reed to commiserate was the worst of it. She couldn't even do so much as call them to make sure they were doing all right.

"I want to do something," Ashlyn exclaimed in anguish, leaning her head back against Keane's chest. He'd made her breakfast this morning after breaking the news to her, but she could barely keep anything down. She'd lost her appetite, but that appeared to be the status quo lately. "I want to talk to Aiden's parents. I want to be with my team. I want this to stop."

"You exposing yourself to the very person who's committing these crimes wouldn't be beneficial in any way to anyone," Keane responded, resting his chin atop of her head. It amazed her that such a beautiful night could be followed up with such tragedy. She pulled his arms tighter around her waist, grateful he was here with her. "You'd become a target and he would do whatever it took to get you in his grasp."

"At least Victor's been cleared of any wrongdoing," Ashlyn offered up, tracing the edges of Keane's watch. She glanced down at the black dialed face, noting it was nothing too fancy. He preferred to dress nice and have nice things, but he never went overboard. She wondered what Keane would think of her dad and then pondered if that would ever happen. They'd agreed to take this day-by-day, but having someone out there killing people and targeting her didn't make that an easy feat. "You mentioned that Mr. Calvert spoke to my father. Are he and my mother doing okay?"

"They're on their way back from Italy." Keane reached for the list of names Coen had given them yesterday. Yesterday? It seemed like they'd been here for weeks. "I keep going over the people who had access to Garner who have the knowledge base to pull off what he's done so far. There are numerous IT technicians on this list, but we know Aiden's key card was used to gain access to the garage."

"Which means the person we're looking for wouldn't be on the list of those who were there at the time. It's mutually exclusive. If he used Aiden's ID to wand into the building, his ID wouldn't be on the list." Ashlyn reached out and took the piece of paper from Keane's hand. She reviewed the names again, noticing that Dennis Paavo wasn't listed. "You mentioned Agent Coulter looked into Dennis. I can't imagine he would do anything like this, but did anything ever come of that?"

Ashlyn loathed that she was actually sorting through the people she worked with like suspects in a novel. It wasn't fair to those who were innocent to have their lives dissected or for them to be interrogated, like Victor, when they'd done nothing wrong.

"Calvert should be in D.C. by now," Keane replied with an underlying confidence in his tone. "I don't know my superior on a personal level all that well, but I can tell you that he won't leave a stone unturned now that he's involved in the investigation. My job? To stay by your side and ensure your safety."

"Adam Walker, one of Bishop Vance's paralegals, isn't on the list." It wasn't that Ashlyn was ignoring what Keane was saying, she was just realizing all the people who could have used Aiden's key card. "And—"

"Ash, you can keep going over and over searching for who wasn't in the building, but you and I know it could easily have been someone already checked into the building." Keane removed the paper from Ashlyn's hand and leaned forward, so that she had to do the same. She crisscrossed her legs and sat facing forward, watching as he folded the list in half. "What about Reed or Parker? What about Paul and his team of technicians? Or Noah, the man who installed the hardware Victor brought over the other night? He isn't accounted for. They all could have easily used Aiden's key card. It could very well be a setup to throw the FBI off of his trail. And you're assuming you know him. It could very well be someone you see in court or the person who delivers your mail to Gina."

Ashlyn gave a small growl of frustration, running her fingers through her hair before pushing herself off of the couch. She'd changed into a pair of shorts and one of her favorite lightweight summer sweaters with the colors of the American flag sewn into the material. She pushed up the quarter-length sleeves and had been about to ask if Keane wanted more coffee when his phone vibrated.

"It's Brody, telling us that Calvert called in Royce. I haven't had the privilege of meeting him yet, but he's the fifth team member and very proficient at this type of investigation." Keane was relaying what was on the display of his phone, using his index finger to scroll through the text. "Well, look at that. It appears Royce worked for the Bureau less than a year back in the day before 9/11. He quit the Bureau and then joined the Marines, serving twelve years before returning home."

"Your team is heavy on the military experience, as well as some civilian law enforcement," Ashlyn said, thankful she had so many people on her side. It still didn't stop her from experiencing guilt for Jarod and Aiden's deaths. No one could take back what happened, even should the FBI or SSI find the man who did this. "I bet this isn't how you pictured your first assignment going."

"No, it isn't," Keane replied with a half-smile, looking up to rest his gaze on her. He set his phone on the coffee table and then stood, walking over to where Ashlyn was aimlessly pacing the floor. He stopped her by placing his hands on her shoulders and forcing her to remain still. "But this first mission gave us another chance, didn't it? We're being given time together when our normal lives wouldn't have ordinarily allowed that. Why don't we spend the afternoon getting to know one another again?"

Ashlyn raised an eyebrow in question, the weight of grief and fear lifting slightly at Keane's sincere smile. He also laughed at her misinterpretation of his proposal.

"I'm not talking about sex, Miss Federal Prosecutor." Keane drifted his fingers over the fabric of her sweater until her hands were in his. The heat they'd created just from touching made her think that maybe they should move this into the bedroom. She'd missed this intimacy. She'd missed him. "I want to get to know you again. I want to know what you've done since we were last together. I'd like to hear about your family, your work, and how you think this might work between us. Let's face it, long distance relationships aren't the easiest."

Ashlyn was keenly aware that Keane was getting her to think of something other than the fact that two people she'd considered friends had been killed. She'd spent more time with Aiden on a daily basis than she did with her parents. She closed her eyes and inhaled deeply, finally accepting that there wasn't anything she could do to change things.

"You're right," Ashlyn agreed, guiding Keane back to the couch. She gave him a gentle push and then sat down in front of him like they'd been positioned before. His arms wrapped around her waist and he rested his cheek against hers. "Tell me how your parents and sister are doing. Are they all still up in Seattle?"

Keane revealed that his mother had passed away three years ago of cancer and then proceeded to tell her about his life in California and his hopes for a new beginning in Florida. Listening to the rich timber of his voice relaxed her and she found herself sharing in his happiness and grief through the stories he told and wishing she'd had the chance to be with him for those experiences...both good and bad.

They spent the rest of the morning and the majority of the afternoon getting caught up, talking and laughing through most of it. They'd made lunch and talked more over the meal, enjoying each other's company. The devastation that had been left in the wake of a killer was always there, just around the corner, but Ashlyn savored this time she'd been given with Keane.

Ashlyn wasn't sure what would happen after this, but she knew without a doubt that she would never be the same. Whether it was due to the realization that she wasn't really living life or the thought that this could all be taken away in the blink of an eye...she finally admitted to wanting more in her life than just a career.

"Sawyer's walking over," Keane said after having looked at his cell phone. They were back on the couch, with her on one end and him on the other. He'd been massaging her foot and she groaned when he stopped, moving her legs to the side so he could sit up. He was wearing a pair of jeans instead of his usual khakis, which he'd thrown in the washing machine earlier this morning. There was no telling how long they would be here. "One of the sensors Coen put in the back isn't connecting to the system. They want to get it up and working before the neighbors arrive home from work."

"You haven't met Sawyer, have you?" Ashlyn asked, tossing her legs over the side of the couch. She reached for her hair tie lying on the coffee table beside the piece of paper Keane had folded earlier. She couldn't help but think the answer lay in that list, but looking at the names only took them in endless circles leading nowhere. "Where is he from?"

"Brody mentioned he was friends with Calvert back in the day, so I'm assuming they were in the same unit," Keane replied, standing and adjusting his shoulder holster. The only time he'd ever taken it off was when they were in bed and she didn't leave the room without her own weapon. Her Px4 Storm was currently within reach on the side table behind her. A knock sounded on the door before she could ask any more questions. "I'll get it."

Keane made his way across the small living room and peered out the side window after having pulled the white curtain to the side. Once he verified who it was—and Ashlyn assumed Keane had been shown Sawyer's picture at some point—he opened the door and stepped back.

"Sawyer," Keane greeted, shaking the man's hand and then shutting the door behind him.

Ashlyn wasn't sure what she was expecting. Maybe she thought he would resemble Coen—tall, dark, and muscular. His black hair and matching eyes made him appear a rather deadly adversary. Keane reminded her of a tiger with his lean build and stunningly perceptive eyes.

Sawyer? He was the boy next door, with the most charming grin Ashlyn had ever seen. The dimple in his right cheek had her returning his smile.

"I think I might want to switch places," Sawyer remarked after sending a wink in Ashlyn's direction. Her smile widened when Keane stepped in front of his teammate and blocked his view. "Or not. I didn't mean anything by that."

Keane lowered his voice to the point where Ashlyn couldn't hear what he had to say to Sawyer, but both men were somewhat more relaxed by the time they turned around to face her.

"Ms. Ellis, it's a pleasure to meet you," Sawyer greeted, stepping forward to shake her hand. "I decided I should come over so you're not subjected to Coen's bad mood. Apparently, the orange juice that was in the refrigerator had his name on it."

Ashlyn laughed and decided that Keane had a good group of men he'd be working with, regardless of Coen's somewhat serious nature. She knew of his brother's troubled past and it couldn't have been easy on his family. She wouldn't mention it again though, because it wasn't her place.

"I think there's an unopened container of orange juice in our refrigerator, if you'd like to take that back as a peace offering," Ashlyn proposed, slipping her hands into the back pockets of her shorts. Keane came to stand beside her, resting his hand on her lower back. It felt somewhat odd to have someone claim her as his, not that she objected. It just felt different. It wasn't something she was used to, which reminded her of the reason they were even here. "Sawyer, thank you for keeping an eye out for us. I feel better knowing someone is watching the outside, even with the bars and all."

"Are you kidding me? When Townes Calvert calls up and offers you the job that dreams are made of, you take it…no questions asked." Sawyer glanced at his watch with a somewhat regretful expression. "I don't have a lot of time. Ms. Hallowell, the neighbor on your left, comes home in about thirty minutes from her job at the post office. She also likes to walk her dog first thing and is quite interested in what goes on in her neighborhood. The last thing we need is for Ms. Hallowell to report a suspicious person in the area to the police."

"Sawyer," Ashlyn said, stopping him when he would have walked past her. "Have you heard anything from my office? Gina is supposed to give Mr. Calvert or Brody updates, but they haven't been in contact with us since this morning."

Sawyer glanced over at Keane, who had now crossed his arms and gave a small nod of encouragement. Their brief conversation by the door hadn't just been about her then. Ashlyn tensed and did her best to brace herself for whatever Sawyer was about to reveal.

"Parker Davis didn't show up for work this morning," Sawyer disclosed reluctantly, as if he hadn't wanted to add to Ashlyn's stress. "He's not at his residence and there was no sign of foul play. Agent Coulter is doing his best to locate him as we speak. Chances are probably that he got spooked and took off for a while to get somewhere safe."

Ashlyn could hear from the tone of Sawyer's voice that no one of authority could verify if Parker was a victim or if they should be looking at him for an entirely different reason. She was physically sick to her stomach at the thought the twenty-nine year old paralegal could have done the vicious and disturbing actions that had been executed within the last few days, let alone what had been done to her. She'd vetted him personally and he had been one of the top students of his law class at George Mason University.

"Parker could just be upset due to Aiden's death," Ashlyn put out there, mostly for her own sense of peace. She wasn't able to hide the hint of desperation. Keane brought her closer to his side. "Agent Coulter might be jumping to conclusions due to Parker's initial background in technology. Look at what happened to Victor. He was interrogated for how long and thought to be the subject we're all looking for, only to be proven innocent. Too many people are being thrown under the bus without enough evidence."

"Ma'am, I understand how frustrating it is to be cooped up in here while not knowing every step the authorities are taking," Sawyer offered, gesturing toward Keane. "His job is to protect you while Coen and I do our best to safeguard the two of you and provide some level of early warning. That's two layers of experienced protection this perpetrator would have to go through should he somehow inadvertently discover your location. I'd say that the chances of that happening were close to impossible, seeing as how you brought nothing with you that had any kind of technology in it for him to track your movements."

Ashlyn was grateful she'd put on the summer sweater instead of the other short-sleeved shirt she'd brought with her. She always kept an extra business suit in her closet, so there hadn't been a need to pack one when they'd decided to stay somewhere else. The chill that invaded her body now wasn't something a piece of clothing could eradicate anyway.

"I really need to speed this up," Sawyer said somewhat apologetically. "I won't be long. Keane, could you let me out the back door?"

Keane let Sawyer out into the backyard and returned to find Ashlyn still standing in the living room with her arms wrapped around herself. He turned her toward him and pulled her into a tight embrace. She rested her cheek against his chest and ran through the last couple of years Parker had been assigned under her supervision. He wasn't the person responsible. She had written several evaluations for pay raises and performance reviews. She knew him really well. She'd been confined to doubting every person she worked with, lived by, or had daily encounters with. It wasn't fair and an anger stirred within her that hadn't been there since the initial break-in.

"We're going to go through every name on that list, those that aren't, and anyone who could have had access to murder Jarod in cold blood without anyone being the wiser," Ashlyn stated with determination, pushing away from Keane and walking over to where the list had been left on the coffee table. She grabbed her pen, got as comfortable as she could on the couch, and started with the first name. "Mia Hernandez."

SHE HAD BEEN *soiled. Taken by a dirty beast who had no more intellect than an animal.*

Ashlyn had been disloyal…to him! How could she have betrayed him like that?

He drummed his fingers on the steering wheel, his anger mounting with each passing mile. The large green sign ahead indicated he had less than thirty miles to drive.

He had her location. It hadn't been all that difficult, really.

He also had the tools he would need in which to take her away from Keane Sanderson. Who did he think he was? He didn't have the right to come into Ashlyn's life and pretend like their past had meaning. It didn't matter to anyone.

His chest burned with the pain Ashlyn had caused. No matter what happened now, it would never be the same. He would never be able to touch her without envisioning the sweaty beast hovering over her or smelling the rancid odor of deceitful sex on her body.

It was appropriate to see the storm clouds gathering outside the windshield. The thunder and lightning would be the perfect cover for what he had planned for this evening. It would take quite a bit of time to dismember the bodies. He had all the information he needed to successfully eliminate those involved in trying to keep Ashlyn from him, but he now had to include her on that list. Only her lifeless body would come with him.

She would join the others in her rightful spot, to join him later in paradise.

CHAPTER SIXTEEN

K EANE WALKED THE inside perimeter of the house checking all the windows and doors as Ashlyn took a hot, steaming shower to ease away the anxiety that had caused nothing but knots in her neck. He offered to give her a deep tissue massage once she was out, but he first wanted to ensure the doors and windows were locked up tight. He also wanted confirmation on the whereabouts of Parker Davis.

"Calvert."

"Any word on Davis?" Keane asked, verifying the deadbolt on the door that led to the backyard.

"No," Townes replied, the quiet in the background telling Keane he was somewhere private. "I'm heading in your direction."

Keane tensed upon hearing Calvert's declaration. He wasn't supposed to be directly involved in the investigations of his team members unless absolutely needed. He hadn't had much of a choice other than to fly into D.C. at the request of the Attorney General, but to then leave the multiple crime scenes to visit a safe house where the subject was currently secured wasn't protocol unless it was warranted.

"Why?"

"Special Agent Coulter's cyber department was able to confirm that the person responsible for hacking into Ms. Ellis' private security system did, in fact, do it from a server inside the U.S. Attorney's Building," Townes conveyed, going into a deeper explanation of how this evidence had been obtained. "Coulter was able to get a search warrant on all the servers utilized in the building based on the access the killer would have had to Jarod Garner's office. There is little doubt that the person responsible for stalking Ms. Ellis and committing multiple murders has administrative access to all those mainframes and a number of other strategically placed systems within the federal service agencies including State, DOJ, and the current Administration."

"Parker Davis didn't have time to slash Garner's throat and get back to his desk without being noticed," Keane explained, having gone over and over this with Ashlyn. "Mia and Parker were at their desks from the moment we called them in to the time Ashlyn discovered Garner's body. He might have gone to the small kitchen on the opposite end of the floor, but it was only to get coffee and he was gone maybe three minutes at best."

"I'm not disagreeing with you, but it goes without saying that he is still missing and no one can locate him. If he shows up there, he has to be detained. Are you one hundred percent certain that Ashlyn didn't take any electronic devices with her— nothing from the office? I had an in-depth conversation with Coulter regarding the timing of things and the fact that this unsub knew exactly who you were and who you worked for. Victor Wright was the only one outside of our circle who was aware SSI was brought in, aside from Ashlyn's team."

Which meant the random text Ashlyn had received regarding Keane's involvement had to have come from someone close to her. Had Parker been able to find time to leave his desk without anyone noticing, take the elevator to a different floor without someone seeing him, and murder Jarod Garner in cold blood? He would have had to take time to clean up as well, considering the mess at the crime scene. Technically, that went to the theory that Parker had nothing to do with stalking Ashlyn or killing two people.

Keane walked over to Ashlyn's briefcase that her father had given her and opened the leather flap. No electronics were found, not even a calculator. Only books and files she'd packed at the last minute. He examined each piece of paper, leather-bound books, and even the worn satchel itself. Nothing stood out and there were no electronics of any kind hidden inside.

"I'm looking at Ashlyn's briefcase now," Keane said, finally putting everything back into place. "There's nothing that would emit a signal of any kind. Let me go and check her personal bag."

It wasn't that Keane thought Ashlyn had purposefully brought something with her, like a cell phone or tablet. For one, she knew better. Two, she was well aware the lengths they were going to in order to keep her safe. She wouldn't jeopardize anyone else's life, let alone her own. Could something have already been in her overnight bag that she wasn't aware of? Such as an iPod? As innocent as an iPod seemed, even that type of technology could be tracked.

"Is there a reason to move locations?" Keane asked, wary of staying in the same place too long if there was any doubt their whereabouts had been compromised. "We can be out of here in under five minutes."

Keane walked down the short hallway, the sounds of the shower coming through the bathroom door. He veered off into the bedroom and picked up Ashlyn's designer duffle bag. Her briefcase, pen, and a few other work items had been hand-medowns—family treasures—but she did have fine taste in other areas of her life.

"I don't want to move Ms. Ellis unless we have a valid reason," Townes stipulated before addressing another drawback. "The subject we're dealing with has access to a variety of specialized equipment. Should he have some type of facial software, the two of you could be located within minutes should you step outside that house. He could use the D.C. area CCTV to locate your whereabouts."

"Agreed," Keane approved, finally zipping up Ashlyn's bag. "Ashlyn has nothing but clothes in her overnight bag. She also has a small toiletry case, but no electronics."

Thunder rumbled above the house, rattling the windows with its deep rolling tenor. It was a good thing they'd made an early dinner—at least, what he could get Ashlyn to eat.

"We're in for some storms tonight, which will make visibility from Coen and Sawyer's vantage point somewhat questionable," Keane stated, walking back out the bedroom, down the small hall, and into the living room. There was a side table against the wall that appeared to hold a few knickknacks. He rummaged around until he found some candles. The generator should kick in if they lose power, but one could never be too careful. "I'll get in contact with them and let them know Davis still hasn't been located and for them to be vigilant."

"I've already taken care of that," Townes advised over what sounded like the rhythm of windshield wipers. He must be closer to Annapolis than he was D.C. "I also have Royce covering her apartment building, watching for anyone who might be looking for her. We have no idea where Parker Davis is or if he's even the person we're looking for. Just stay alert and call for backup if you feel there's a problem. I should be there within the hour."

Keane wrapped up the phone call and then walked into the kitchen. There was a small storage room off of the pantry where emergency supplies were kept. Sure enough, a couple of flashlights were positioned on the middle shelf. He picked them up and pressed the buttons on each, confirming they were in working order and the batteries had plenty of life left in them. He had one in his go-bag, but it never hurt to have more on hand.

Another round of thunder boomed loudly above the house, but a quick glance outside showed the lightning didn't streak the sky until at least thirty seconds later. The eye of the storm was still quite a few miles away. He went back into the living room to find Ashlyn walking down the hallway in a white pullover shirt with a pair of blue jean shorts. They would both be washing clothes come morning, granted that they still had power.

"Everything okay?" Ashlyn asked, using the white terry-cloth towel in her hands to dry the long strands of chestnut brown hair already curling into the loose waves he loved. Keane didn't answer right away, standing there in somewhat awe of the fact that they'd found each other again. They would take things slow and try to get things right this time, although that couldn't happen unless they started living their regular lives. Keane had to trust in Agent Coulter's ability to locate the person responsible for all of this carnage. "I thought I heard your voice."

"I was talking to Calvert," Keane admitted, setting the two flashlights on the coffee table. He was aware she'd taken her weapon into the bathroom with her, but he didn't see it now. "Where is your firearm?"

Ashlyn didn't so much as roll her eyes, but the look she gave him was one of disbelief. She reached for her hip, turning forward enough so that he could see she was wearing the small black clip-on holster Coen had brought her yesterday.

She was a pool of contradictions. She was a top-notch federal prosecutor in the courtroom that no one in their right mind wanted on their bad side, appearing every bit of a professional career woman as those who came before her. Now? She looked younger than her thirty-some years, baring no make-up with her naturally flushed cheeks and rosy lips. Her blue eyes practically dared him to make a comment, for which he was smart enough to stick to the topic at hand.

"Calvert is driving here tonight. He should arrive within the hour," Keane admitted, walking over to the chair where his go-bag was currently seated. He was able to move it from room to room, taking with him the weapons and equipment needed should someone try to break into the house. "Parker Davis is still MIA. Calvert isn't comfortable with all of the open-ended guesses being circulated. Since the Attorney General personally called in SSI to oversee your protection—and now to get involved in the investigation—Calvert isn't leaving anything to chance."

"You do know this isn't about the Attorney General, right?" Ashlyn asked, moving farther into the room and taking a seat on the couch as she continued to towel dry her hair. "All of this pressure is because of my father and his friends in positions of power and influence. He's scared for me and putting pressure on those who still owe him favors."

"I suspected as much," Keane said as another clap of thunder sounded above them. He took out the LED flashlight he'd used for years and checked it for service. "One of the reasons Calvert started his own firm was so that he could oversee operations, not take part in them."

"I know we said we wouldn't rush into anything, but have you thought about what happens after this?" Ashlyn asked, her blue eyes never once lifting off of Keane's face. She lowered the towel and sat forward on the edge of the couch, her need to describe to him what she'd felt was evident. "When you told me to leave my laptop back at the office, I hesitated. Everything I am is wrapped up in that square device. Everything, Keane. I realized I hadn't had dinner with my friends in probably nine months. I hadn't spoken to anyone other than my colleagues or my parents in the same amount of time as well. I finally got what I've worked so hard for and…"

Keane caught Ashlyn's hand as it waved in the air, demonstrating that nothing she'd done had garnered her true happiness. He pressed his lips to the back of her fingers, sitting on the coffee table across from her. He set the flashlight beside him, giving him time to formulate his words.

"I should never have let you walk away from me in California," Keane admitted candidly, resting his elbows on his knees while never releasing her hand. He leaned forward enough so that their faces were inches apart and she couldn't misunderstand a thing he said. "We were on different paths and instead of creating a new one, we both went our separate ways. We were wrong. I don't think a day has passed that your face hasn't appeared in my mind or memories from the time we shared together didn't replay over in my dreams. I don't want to live like that…the not knowing what could have been. Do I have all of the answers right now? No. But whatever happens, we'll figure it out together."

"Is it wrong that I'm afraid we won't get to see that?" Ashlyn whispered, right before the lights flickered. The thunder was becoming louder and the lightning was even closer. "I don't want—"

Darkness descended as the lights went out. The generator should kick in any moment…

CHAPTER SEVENTEEN

A SHLYN WAITED FOR the electricity to come back on, but she realized they weren't going to be that lucky after listening for a few seconds of pounding rain without hearing the generator kick in. Keane released her hand and reached for the flashlight, providing them enough illumination of the living room. She reached out for one of the other flashlights, wrapping her fingers around the cold handle.

"We needed a little mood lighting, anyway," Ashlyn murmured, glancing toward the front window. Well, maybe not this kind of ambiance. It was pitch black outside, with the exception of when lightning would streak across the sky. The curtains couldn't hide the bright light that lit up the night every now and then. "It's either that or maybe fate doesn't want us to have that conversation."

"Hey," Keane admonished, capturing a kiss before he stood and pulled his phone out of the front pocket of his jeans. "Fate might have had a hand in having our paths cross once again, but it's up to us to do something about it once we're given the opportunity. As for the electricity, the generator should kick on if they have kept up on the maintenance."

Ashlyn sighed and set her flashlight in her lap as she picked up the damp towel, resuming rubbing her long hair with the soft fabric. She had been going to return to the bathroom and use the blow dryer underneath the sink, but that was out of the question now. She observed Keane as he made a call, wondering why she felt the instinctive urge to look around the house. The generator should have started up by this point. The only noise was that of the storm and it was unsettling, as not even the hum of the air conditioning could be heard anymore. It was as if the house had died.

Keane initiated a conversation with Coen regarding the loss of electricity, the apparent issue with the generator, and also the fact that it appeared as if the entire block had lost power. At least, that was what Ashlyn interpreted from what she could hear on this end. They believed it was nothing to be concerned about, though it did take the alarm system out and the wireless router, which connected a number of wireless sensors. Coen and Sawyer would be forced to observe the property from their location across the street. They spoke of check-in times and perimeter searches, leaving Ashlyn to wonder if Agent Coulter had ever located Parker. She was worried about him. She believed in his innocence, just as she'd believed in Victor's. It wasn't long before Keane disconnected the call, slipping his cell into his front pocket.

"It looks like we might not have electricity for the night, unless we do something to fix the generator," Keane said, looking around the living room. His lips thinned slightly as he voiced what Ashlyn was thinking. "Sawyer is headed outside now to see why the backup generator hasn't kicked on."

"What's the temperature outside?" Ashlyn asked, guessing it was in the high sixties this time of night. She set the damp towel on the side table. They'd be fine until daybreak, but they'd have to open some windows come tomorrow morning. She wasn't so sure Keane would agree to that. "We can make it for a while without old sparky."

"That's not the point," Keane said, the issue with the genera-tor obviously bothering him more than he let on. Ashlyn absolutely hated that nauseous reaction her stomach immediately gave with his unease. She grabbed the flashlight and stood, wanting to be ready for anything. "I checked over the house after we entered and I know the brand of the generator installed. It should have kicked on without a problem. It's a recent installation and the indicator was green."

"Are you saying—"

"I'm saying Sawyer is going to take a look and we'll have more answers after that." Keane motioned for Ashlyn to follow behind him before making his way to the kitchen. From there, they should be able to see where the generator was currently positioned on a concrete slab at the back of the lot. She should know. She'd done the perimeter walk with him, seeing as Coen and Sawyer hadn't arrived until later that day. Keane had refused to leave her alone inside a house without protection. "Stay inside the doorframe so you have a visual of both entry points and the garage entry directly in front of you."

Ashlyn placed her flashlight between her knees before piling her damp hair on top of her head. She then pulled the hair tie off of her wrist and wrapped it around the bundle of strands, before repeating the action two more times until her hair was secure. She didn't want it in the way should they need to run. She then grabbed her flashlight and pointed it toward the living room. She found herself thinking about drawing her weapon.

Run?

Ashlyn wasn't sure where she'd gotten that notion. Keane wasn't the type to run, and technically neither was she. It was the darkness that unnerved her as she observed the beam of Keane's light as he made his way past the kitchen table to the back door.

He aimed the bright lone ray toward the floor as he maneuvered his back toward the wall and tried to get a visual of the generator.

Neither spoke, making the atmosphere all that more tense. Ashlyn tried to convince herself they had nothing to worry about. After all, she'd left all of her electronics either back at home or at her office. No one knew where she was and that was when she recalled a story her father had told her once when she'd been a little girl.

The darkness brings out one's fear of what he or she cannot control. Imagine there is light. Now what do you see?

It hadn't worked then and it wasn't working now. Her father had tried his best to get her past that stage of being afraid of the dark, but it had taken years. Maybe she hadn't truly gotten over that fear, because her heart rate was accelerating and the palms of her hands were starting to perspire.

Ashlyn wiped her left palm down her shorts and then did the same with her right. She repeatedly swung her gaze between Keane and the living room, where she had a good view of the front door. It did cross her mind that should someone want in, all they would have had to do was break a window in the bedroom and somehow get past the bars. But they would have heard the shattering of glass, right? She swung the beam toward the hallway.

"It's pitch black outside with the exception of when lightning streaks across the sky." It was more than evident Keane didn't like the fact that Sawyer was outside without backup. He stepped away from the back door and then joined her, indicating she should go back into the living room. He waited until they were by the couch, but he was foolish if he thought she could sit down. He pulled out his cell phone, connecting to the person he sought. "Coen, it's hard for me to get a visual out the back. The generator is up against the right backside of the lot, out of my line of sight behind the shed."

Ashlyn held her breath as she tried to hear Coen's voice on the other end of the line. She couldn't make out his words clearly and had to rely on Keane's answers to decipher the conversation. She set the flashlight on its base, so that the beam was illuminating a wider space.

"Okay," Keane replied to something Coen said. There was a tightness in his hard tone that told her all she needed to know. "Tell him to stay in contact though. I don't like the fact that we don't have a visual of the back of the property."

Ashlyn picked up the matches that were next to some candles and tore one of the thick sticks out of the small booklet. She ran the bulbous head over the black strip, initiating a spark before she held the small flame to the wick of the first candle. She proceeded to light each one individually until all three were lit, wishing she hadn't completed the task so fast.

"Sawyer's headed out the door now," Keane informed Ashlyn, not telling her anything she hadn't interpreted for herself. She picked up one of the candles and slowly walked toward the kitchen, sensing him behind her with each step. She set the candle down in the middle of the table and then rubbed the palms of her hands down the front of her shorts once again. She inhaled deeply to calm her racing heart. "Let's go back into the living room."

"It could be something simple, right?" Ashlyn inquired, thinking of a million reasons why the generator wasn't working. "Think about it. Coen and Sawyer have been watching this place twenty-four seven in shifts. No one could have gotten near the house without them noticing."

"You're right, but that doesn't mean we're going to take that point zero one percent chance." Keane rested a hand on

Ashlyn's lower back as they walked to the couch. His touch encouraged her to relax, but it was his words that had her anxiety lessening. "Sawyer will get the generator up and running. Until then, we'll keep each other company."

"It's a good thing I like you or you might be in trouble now," Ashlyn said with a small smile, appreciating what he was trying to do. She truly wished Keane would sit on the couch with her, but he remained standing in a manner that gave him a view of all access points. He hadn't laughed at her small joke, leaving her somewhat bereft. Thirty seconds passed, and then another thirty. The sound of her own breathing was becoming somewhat maddening. "You're not being such good company…just saying."

Keane lifted one side of his mouth in a smirk and gave a small shake of his head. Ashlyn smiled as the tension in her shoulders eased with the light talk. She leaned back and tucked her legs underneath her, utilizing their time together for some small talk. She'd been wondering about something and she might as well ask while they had time to kill.

"Do you get frequent flyer miles?" Ashlyn asked, resting her elbow on the back of the couch. She had to believe that Sawyer would get the generator up and running, just as she had to trust that their location hadn't been compromised. She'd done everything Keane had asked of her. "I mean, think of all the perks we can rack up from the mileage."

"Are you willing to give up your weekends and possibly some weekdays?" Keane asked now that Ashlyn had finally caught his attention. His dark gaze didn't contain one gold fleck from where she was seated. The intensity heated her blood and reminded her of what she'd given up all those years ago. "Our schedules won't always coincide and we certainly don't work the average forty-hour week."

"No, we don't," Ashlyn concurred softly, watching as the candlelight flickered across Keane's features. His expression gave nothing away. She took the first step, her heart racing now for a totally different reason. "I woke up this morning to find your eyes closed right in front of me. I don't think you were sleeping, but I laid still so you wouldn't know I was watching you. I used to do that before, but then it dawned on me that it was for a totally different reason."

Keane continued to watch Ashlyn with curiosity, although he didn't ask about her objective. They *had* changed from their time together. They were both older, wiser, and at a different place in their lives where their priorities had changed. This horrific situation had opened her eyes in a manner she was afraid to admit might not have happened until it was too late.

"I didn't need to memorize the way your lashes curved or the shape of your lips," Ashlyn continued, needing Keane to know she wasn't going to change her mind this time. "I didn't need to imprint anything to memory, because I could see it every day. I don't need to sacrifice a part of myself to serve the justice system. I don't want to be like Jarod…living, breathing, and dying at his desk. I—"

Keane was in front of Ashlyn before she could finish her next sentence. He pulled her forward, causing her to unfold her legs and lean into his warmth. He pressed a tender kiss to her forehead and then pulled back so that they weren't more than inches apart.

"You will *not* end up like Jarod Garner," Keane whispered harshly, as if to imprint those words in her mind. His belief that everything would turn out okay and that they would finally have a chance to get things right had her throat tightening with emotion. She so wanted to believe him, but this constant fear had chipped away at her defenses. "We have a future together,

Ash. We do. We'll figure things out as each day passes and—"

Ashlyn inhaled sharply at the sound of Keane's phone vibrating in his pocket. He squeezed her hand before releasing his hold on her and answering the call. Her chest constricted when she comprehended his reply.

"One tango?"

Keane disconnected, pulled Ashlyn off of the couch, and withdrew the firearm from his holster simultaneously and without pause. She reached for her own weapon, palming the Px4 Storm. Why didn't she feel safer?

"Coen confirmed Sawyer made it to the back of the house, but he isn't checking in." Keane took Ashlyn by the hand and guided her around the couch, toward the hallway. "Someone is approaching the front door. I want you in the bathroom, deadbolt latched. Coen's coming our way now. You don't open that door for anyone but us."

"What?" Ashlyn whispered, not really knowing why since Keane hadn't lowered his voice. "I'm not leaving you to—"

A resounding knock came on the door.

"Now, Ashlyn," Keane instructed briskly, releasing her hand and then starting for the front door. There wasn't a chance in hell she was going down that hall without a flashlight. Technically, she wasn't going to lock herself up in some small room trapped while Keane was out here by himself with no backup. Was Sawyer lying dead somewhere? How soon before Coen made it across the street? "Do as I say!"

"And what if someone comes through the other entrance?" Ashlyn pointed out harshly, not willing to leave the safety of Keane's side. She positioned herself against the wall, giving herself the advantage when the lights finally flickered…only to go out once again. "I'm safer here."

Keane was shaking his head in disagreement, but he didn't

have time to argue when another blow came on the door. The wood shook from the strength of the action. Who took the time to knock and give themselves away? This wasn't making any sense and it was evident Keane was thinking the same thing. He still didn't answer, most likely delaying long enough for Coen to reach them. Keane's sharp gaze swung to hers when a voice called out.

"Ashlyn, it's me! It's Parker. Open up!"

HE SMILED AS he stood over the man's body. The electric shock Sawyer Madison had received was enough to stop his heart, given the fact that he hadn't been well grounded standing in that puddle. At least, he thought it was Madison. It could easily be Coen Flynn, but that didn't matter. One was as good as another.

He didn't take time to feel for a pulse, knowing this would be over in a matter of minutes. He would eliminate those who stood in his way and then put Ashlyn Ellis with the others—where she had always belonged.

He lifted his face to the rain and opened his mouth, allowing the fresh liquid to slide down his throat. The cleansing this night had offered him was most welcome. He then tilted his head, listening for the sound of his cue.

CHAPTER EIGHTEEN

K EANE DIDN'T LIKE the loss of positive control and the fact that his backup wasn't interfering with a suspect currently trying to gain access through the front door of the safe house. Sawyer should have easily observed Parker Davis in the vicinity, although the flickering lights indicated one of the support team agents was working on the generator at the back of the property. Why, then, hadn't he answered Coen's call? Nothing was adding up the way it should.

Sawyer should have easily heard Parker call out, thus making his way back to the front of the house. The only thing to prevent that from happening was if the two had gotten into a confrontation, ending in a manner where Davis had the upper hand, however unlikely that might seem.

"Keane?"

Ashlyn had whispered his name, but he put a finger to his lips. He needed to decide how to handle this in the most effective manner. Leaving Davis outside where no one could see him or control him wasn't a viable option. A visual of the target was essential, but where the hell was Coen? He should have crossed the street by now and been able to eliminate or detain this potential threat.

"Parker, put your hands on your head," Keane barked

through the thick wood, staying to the left side of the entrance after removing the barricade bar. He rested his finger on the trigger and wrapped his left hand around the brass knob of the deadbolt for the door. "Face out toward the street."

"What?" Parker called out, genuine confusion lacing his tone. "I—"

"Do as I said or I'll shoot you where you stand," Keane ordered loudly, doing a sweep of their surroundings. It didn't appear anyone had broken in from the back, but this could very well be a distraction. Things weren't adding up and that only enhanced the dangerous position they were in. "Now!"

"Fine!" Parker called out over the resounding crack of thunder. "I'm facing the street."

Keane swung the door open, already having raised his weapon and was in position to fire. Parker Davis stood on the porch as instructed, his fingers laced behind his head. Rain was pounding the ground and the small overhead structure didn't prevent Davis from getting the brunt of the volley.

Keane wasn't about to make himself a target by stepping outside to pat Davis down for weapons, so he did the only thing he could.

"Take two steps back and then close the door," Keane instructed, motioning for Ashlyn that she shouldn't say a word. Davis couldn't see her presence from where he was standing and it was going to stay that way until Keane was able to sort through the events. He peered over Davis' shoulder, but he wasn't able to see too far into the darkness before the door finally closed. Where the hell was Coen? "Lock the deadbolt, put your hands on the door, and spread your legs."

Davis was wearing a pair of cargo shorts and a basic black T-shirt, both of which were soaked. The candlelight wasn't much, but it was enough to see that droplets of water were hitting the hardwood floor, as well as dripping from the man's hair. Keane stepped forward and patted him down, looking for any type of weapon he could have on his person. Surprisingly, the man was totally unarmed.

Keane slowly walked around Davis to the left, leaving a wide berth and ensuring that Davis' attention was on him and him alone. This position gave Keane a vantage point of the room, while maintaining an eye on Ashlyn and the two other entrances. He maintained the sight of his weapon on the widest point of his target.

"Answer the questions in order," Keane ordered firmly, with no hesitation. He didn't care that Davis appeared nervous and terrified. He'd get over it if he wasn't the man Coulter was looking for. "How did you know we were here? Why are you here? And who else is with you?"

"I-I got Ashlyn's message," Parker said, about to lower his hands when Keane motioned that he should put his hands up and lace his fingers behind his head. "She told me to come here without telling anyone, only saying that she was in danger. I'm here by myself. I swear."

Keane never took his eyes off of Davis as he pulled his phone out of his pocket and redialed. Coen's line rang continuously without answer. Shit. He then tried to get ahold of Calvert, but Keane's attempt only garnered the same result. He then dialed 911, allowing the line to remain open for the authorities to trace their location.

"Parker, I didn't bring my cell phone with me," Ashlyn said with caution, causing Keane to shake his head at her attempt to gather information. He hadn't wanted her presence known and lifted his weapon a fraction of an inch to warn Davis that he shouldn't turn around or look in her direction. It worked well enough when he saw the big .45 caliber barrel pointed between his eyes, garnering his whole attention. "I told you that before I left the office, so why would you believe I sent you a message like that? Do you know Agent Coulter is looking for you?" Davis had now started to shake at what Keane presumed was the realization that he was in a shitload of trouble. His lips parted as if he was going to speak, but Ashlyn couldn't see that and talked over him.

"Did you kill Chief Garner and Aiden?" Even Keane could hear the tremor in Ashlyn's voice. He wanted to spare her this, but they needed answers...fast. Staying here wasn't an option, but Keane needed to clear a space for them to leave. That wasn't going to be easy without knowing what awaited them outside in the darkness. "Are you the one who's been stalking me?"

"What?" Parker said with disbelief, most likely wanting to turn around to confront the accusation. He made the smart decision and remained where he was. "I swear, Ashlyn, I didn't kill anyone! You know me, for Christ's sake. I haven't done anything wrong. I got your message right after hearing about Aiden. Your message said that we were both in danger and that I needed to meet you here. I'm not stupid enough to fall for something like that without confirmation, so I asked for a response to a question to verify that it was you. You replied with something only you and I would know."

"You're going to have to clarify that," Keane instructed in a steel tone, needing this conversation to hurry along. Two of his teammates weren't answering, his boss was no longer answering his cell phone, and a killer had possibly just caught them in a trap. "Parker?"

"Ashlyn texted me something only the two of us would know, confirming it was her." It was more than evident Davis wanted to turn around and plead with Ashlyn to believe him, but he made the wise choice and remained facing Keane. The two candles didn't give off nearly enough light, but it wasn't hard to read the man's body language as he tried to keep from pissing himself. Davis turned his head just enough to speak with Ashlyn out of the corner of his mouth. "Your message stated I came to you last week with a request for time off, because I wanted to finally take the bar exam. No one knew that except you."

"Where did this conversation take place?" Keane asked, hoping to get the answer he wanted. Ashlyn's apartment had been monitored with listening and audio devices, but her office had been swept clean. Parker appeared to be waiting for Ashlyn to respond. "Davis, answer the question."

"Um, her office at work." Davis shifted his stance. His arms were likely starting to burn from maintaining his position, but that was too damn bad. "I waited until I knew for sure she had time to discuss it."

"Was Ashlyn's office door closed?" Keane asked, needing a quick answer. Where the hell were the cops?

"Yes, yes," Parker responded, not knowing he'd just thrown a wrench into the working gears Keane and SSI had put into place.

"Ashlyn, you were swept for bugs and tracking devices, as was the additional apparel you brought with you," Keane said, lowering his weapon and taking his finger off of the trigger. Davis was a pawn—nothing more and nothing less. "This perp isn't just tracking you, he has somehow been able to listen in on your conversations even in situations where he shouldn't have had access. Think, Ash. How is that possible?"

Keane might have ruled Davis out as a suspect, but damned if he would turn his back on an unknown subject whose alliances were unclear. Her bag had already been checked and so had her briefcase, but what if there was something inside that had been missed? He walked over to where Ashlyn had set the satchel down in the chair, the flap already lifted. He used his flashlight to look inside, tracing his fingers over the lining of the leather. He then pulled everything out of the bag, looking at the spine of the two books and dumping the contents of the folders on the ground. Nothing.

"Oh my God," Ashlyn whispered in revulsion, taking a tentative step forward to where she'd set some of her things on the coffee table. She went to reach for something when Keane stopped her. He stared at the silver Mont Blanc Meisterstuck pen that had been handed down two generations. "He's been listening to us this entire time."

A gunshot rang out before Keane could examine the pen, not that confirmation was needed. It was more than apparent that they'd been hunted in a manner typical of a coward. This man hid behind his technology, stalking and terrorizing a woman and then murdering those associated with her from behind. They'd been found and were now cornered, but that by no means meant they had been defeated. Now that they could confront their attacker, he would have to show himself to get what he wanted.

"Ashlyn, you and Parker lock yourselves in the bathroom right now," Keane instructed against his own wishes, not wanting to leave her side, but knowing it was for the best. He had to believe this wasn't the last time he'd see her, touch her, tell her he—fuck it. Why not? He grabbed the flashlight she'd left on the coffee table and quickly escorted them down the short hallway. He wasn't going to take the chance that they could be ambushed through the bedroom window. Ashlyn spun around and he pressed the metal handle into her hand, wrapping his fingers around the back of her neck. "I love you. Shoot first, ask questions later. Got it?"

"Yeah," Ashlyn whispered before kissing him almost desperately. He tore away from her, knowing they were fighting for time and space to live. He just hoped like hell it had been Coen firing that shot and not the other way around. "I got it. And Keane? I love you, too."

CHAPTER NINETEEN

A SHLYN CLOSED AND bolted the door behind Keane, already knowing it was the wrong decision. She leaned her head against the wood and strained to listen for any sounds that would indicate a struggle. She was sending the man she loved—the one she walked away from five years ago—into a situation more dangerous than the one they'd already been through. She couldn't let him do this alone if there was a chance she could alter the outcome.

"Parker, take these." Ashlyn had made a decision and nothing could change her mind. She spun on the heel of her bare foot and shoved the flashlight into his chest. The look of horror on Parker's face said it all, but she wouldn't allow that to alter her decision. She grabbed his other hand and pressed her weapon firmly into his palm. "You heard Keane. You shoot anyone who tries to come in here that isn't him or me. Do you understand?"

"You can't go out there unarmed," Parker whispered, trying to give back the items she'd already given him. He was also shaking his head to back up his claim, although that might have been shivering due to his wet clothes, which were now most likely cold. "Are you insane? Chief Garner is dead, and so is Aiden. This man is a killer. Let the professionals handle this. We can—"

"Parker, I'm your boss," Ashlyn stated firmly, done having this conversation. Parker was in his late twenties, but he was still quite young and idealistic. The good guys didn't always get the bad guys. "You do as I tell you. Stay here, lock the door behind me, and shoot anyone who tries to get in here that isn't one of us."

Ashlyn didn't give Parker time to argue. She'd known he wasn't a person who could take another's life. He didn't have it in him and she trusted her instincts. She turned around and unfastened the deadbolt, opening the door quicker than she'd intended. She hadn't wanted Parker to stop her, but she needed to be more careful in her actions. The hallway was dark, especially since she'd left the flashlight with Parker. She didn't move right away, listening for him to lock up after her and also to ensure that she was alone.

Silence.

Ashlyn quietly proceeded down the short hallway, using her hand against the wall to guide her toward the living room. The candles were still lit; giving enough illumination that she could see no one was in the room with her. The front door was barred once again. Keane must have gone out either the back or the garage. The second flashlight was right there on the coffee table, so she quickly grabbed it before backtracking her steps to the bedroom. The black duffel bag that Coen had given them was stashed under the bed with additional weapons. She couldn't go outside empty-handed. She needed another pistol.

It took Ashlyn less than thirty seconds to locate the bag and obtain the small handgun she already knew how to operate. She shoved the bag back where she'd found it and then clicked the flashlight off, plunging herself back into darkness. She retraced her steps, once again using the wall as guidance, and made her way back through the living room.

The gunshot had come from the back and that was the direction Keane must have gone as well. Ashlyn would be better off going out the front door and making her way around the side of the house, thus giving her the element of surprise. It dawned on her that had she been alone, she never would have been brave enough to do this, but she didn't stop to think about it. She couldn't, or else she wouldn't have been able to remove the bar and unlock the deadbolt, before turning the handle to step out into the rain.

The thunder and lightning appeared to have moved to the east, but the rain was relentlessly pouring down without an end in sight. The sky was pitch black and so was the street. Ashlyn tried to peer across, looking for any sign of Coen and Sawyer. No movement whatsoever ahead of her. She stepped off of the porch and veered left, listening closely for any sound of someone approaching. The only thing she heard was the thud of the raindrops hitting the ground, drowning out any other noise.

The wet grass was cold on Ashlyn's bare feet, but she didn't stop until she came to the cherry tree at the corner of the garage. She thought about walking around it, but then figured *he* might see her. She also didn't want Keane to accidentally think she was the intruder and shoot her on sight. She dipped underneath the branches and managed to get closer to the edge of the house. The dampness made it hard to breathe, as it brought the mildew smell up from the deep-rooted tree and old musty mulch surrounding its base.

Ashlyn looked back, wiping the rain from her eyes. She could barely see ten feet in front of her or behind, but she could have sworn she saw a shadow across the street move toward her, and go in between the houses. Coen? She couldn't be positive, but she wasn't about to backtrack and make herself a viable target.

Another gunshot rang out and she literally jumped, raising a hand to her chest as fear sliced through her. What if *he* had shot Keane? The graphic vision she'd conjured up was enough to encourage her to move, putting one foot in front of another as she rounded the corner of the house. Why was it that it appeared darker here? There was roughly twenty feet from where she was to the neighbor's home, with bushes forming a hedge line separating the properties.

The rain was still coming down as Ashlyn continued to slowly make her way to the back of the property. She'd only made it halfway when she heard Keane's voice, talking in a rather soothing manner. Had he discovered Sawyer and was telling him help was on the way? Was it Coen? She took a few more steps to try and see who it was, but she also didn't want to call attention to herself.

Ashlyn would have screamed had she had the time, but instead she was literally shoved into the concrete of the garage wall, unarmed, with a hand over her mouth to prevent her from shouting for help before she could do a damn thing.

"Shhhh." Ashlyn couldn't make out the man's features, but she instinctively knew she didn't know him. He was massive, as in those fighters on television. His shoulders had to be at least twice the length of hers and she unconsciously brought her knee up with enough force to inflict damage, but the man didn't budge. Panic took hold and she struggled, only to find that he pressed his body harder against hers and whispered in her ear. "Ms. Ellis. I'm Townes Calvert. I need you to stop fighting and run as fast as you can across the street, to where Coen and Sawyer were setup above the garage."

Ashlyn was already shaking her head, refusing to leave Keane behind. He was with Sawyer or Coen, but one of them needed medical attention. The gunshots said it all and she wasn't about to leave without doing what she could to help. It was because of her they were hurt.

"You tainted her," a voice shrieked aloud, causing Ashlyn to go absolutely still. It was enough for Townes to slowly release his hold on her, but he didn't understand. She couldn't have heard right. There had to be some mistake. "She was mine. For months, she paid attention to me—smiling, laughing, and even touching me. You ruined her and then turned her against me. So you're going to go in there and get her or I will put a bullet in your friend's head and then yours."

"You know how this is going to end," Keane replied quietly, doing his best to soothe Andrew Rutledge while dissuading him from following through with whatever delusion he'd convinced himself he was living out. Ashlyn was grateful the concrete kept her upright or otherwise her trembling knees would have given out on her. She fought off the nausea as it rose in her throat, burning all the way. A man she'd considered a colleague, a friend, had invaded her privacy by watching her twenty-four hours a day in her own home. A man who killed two people they'd both known. Two men she admired greatly, both of which would have had long lives ahead of them if it hadn't been for this sad, delusional man. "You can't get away with this, Andrew. Too many people are now involved and you've made a lot of mistakes. The best thing you can do right now is lower that weapon and give yourself up before you force my hand."

The two men continued to exchange words while Townes Calvert maintained his stance on Ashlyn leaving the scene. She couldn't, not with Keane's life on the line and whomever Andrew was threatening to kill. She dug her heels into the grass and tugged against Towne's grip when he tried to extract her from the situation.

"He'll listen to me," Ashlyn whispered in encouragement, doing her best to get Townes on her side without him hearing the fear consuming her. She managed to grab ahold of him, unable to wrap her fingers completely around his forearm. "Please. I can talk him down without anyone else getting hurt."

Even through the darkness, Ashlyn could see the large man shake his head in disagreement. Desperation clawed at her and she took a hold of that, spinning it into what she dealt with on a daily basis when she spent hours convincing a jury of someone's guilt.

"Mr. Calvert, I'm the only one who can get your man out of this situation," Ashlyn stated persuasively, straightening her shoulders and pushing against him to garner some room so that she could at least look up into his face. The shadows prevented her from seeing his features, but she conjured up what she thought he might look like. "Andrew Rutledge is a colleague and one I know rather well. He won't hurt me, but he's already proved that he's willing to kill for me. Let me talk him down while you figure out a way to stop him from killing anyone else. I can at least give you the time to do that much."

Ashlyn waited, fighting the urge to try and run toward Keane. That would likely end up resulting in more deaths, so she maintained her composure and hoped like hell Townes agreed with her assessment of the situation. For whatever reason, Andrew wasn't in a position to be eliminated. She understood how these situations worked better than anyone. Keane would have taken the shot already if he could and Townes Calvert knew that.

"We do this my way," Townes conceded in a tone Ashlyn wasn't so sure was on purpose. He sounded as if he'd had trauma to his voice box, but that wasn't her concern. He also had strung along a line of curse words she hadn't even known existed. He wasn't happy with her plan, but it appeared it was all they had at the moment. "Announce yourself first. Stay away from Keane, giving him a chance to do what he does best. He'll know I'm around to cause a distraction when he needs it, so keep Rutledge occupied, but stay out of his line of sight. And for Christ's sake, you run as fast as you can if you so much as think he's coming after you. Got it?"

Townes Calvert wasn't the most polished speaker, but he certainly got his point across. Ashlyn was so relieved he was allowing her to do this that she didn't give him a chance to renege or let herself think about the risk she was taking. It was nowhere near the danger Keane was currently standing in and trying to talk his way out. She managed to get to the back of the house and looked over her shoulder, only to find that Townes wasn't anywhere in sight. For someone so large, he could move quickly and remain undetected in an alarmingly short amount of time.

"You have on the count of three to retrieve Ashlyn and—"

"I'm here," Ashlyn called out, wiping the rain away in hopes that would make her see better. It didn't. The tree line in the back made it even harder to make out the figures, but she could distinguish Keane next to the generator. Townes' cautionary word on giving Keane space to do his job came to mind, so she stayed where she was and ignored the sharp inhalation that had come from someone near Keane's position. Was Andrew holding someone hostage? Coen and Sawyer were nowhere to be found. "Andrew, what's going on?"

"Don't act like you don't know," Andrew shouted, sounding nothing like the professional prosecutor she'd dealt with numerous times in the past. Ashlyn was starting to understand how witnesses always stated under oath that they had no knowledge of previous behavior issues. And it wasn't only those types of questions they couldn't answer. It was looking back and then seeing the signs of something he or she could have stopped. She could honestly say now that she could see his ability to pull something like this off. Andrew was assigned the Haung case because of his technical comprehension, but no one had really known the extent of his knowledge. Now they did, but it was a little too late. "You said yourself that we were soul mates. You made me believe you, but you're just like all the rest. You're a filthy whore and I should have known you weren't worthy of my affection from the beginning."

Ashlyn only now caught on to the fact that she could do nothing to prevent Andrew from killing more innocent people. Whoever he had with him in the tree line was going to be shot to death because she'd realized too late that her presence had only aggravated him. She'd read the situation wrong and had put all of them in more danger, if that were even possible. She needed to turn the tables or else the person Andrew had would be dead within a minute. She hoped like hell Keane understood what she was about to do. She could either beg Andrew for forgiveness or she could anger him in a manner that would create the response they needed. She chose the latter.

"Worthy of your affection? You've got to be kidding me, right?" Ashlyn spat out in disgust, hoping she carried off her revulsion credibly. If she could only get him to step out far enough for Keane to distinguish between the shadows of the trees and Andrew's silhouette, they all might stand a chance of getting out of this alive. "Andrew, what you've done disgusts me. I wouldn't allow you touch me if you were the last man on earth and I certainly wouldn't—"

Ashlyn was once again hit, although this time from behind. She hadn't been paying attention and the resulting damage was her now lying in the wet grass without the ability to breathe. She tried to scramble away, hearing shouts from various positions around the property. Terror flooded her system as she looked up just in time to see the firing of a weapon...aimed directly at Keane.

NONE OF THEM *deserved to live.*

Rage and fury like he'd never known caused him to react without thinking it out, something he'd never done before. He was running on pure emotion and it felt incredible. It was almost as if he were undergoing an out-of-body experience. A euphoric high embraced him and he became invincible.

He raised his weapon and continued firing until everything went dark.

CHAPTER TWENTY

KEANE HAD ONLY ever experienced fear like this once before…and both times had been due to Ashlyn being in the line of fire. She'd purposefully stepped into Rutledge's line of sight, exposing herself to the whims of an insane killer who had been brutally obsessed with her for close to a year. How did Keane know this? Because Rutledge had gleefully described in detail his fascination of his colleague.

What were innocent, casual gestures to Ashlyn had meant much more to Andrew Rutledge, who clearly thought he was the sane one among them. He saw nothing wrong with what he'd done or the fact that he'd killed two innocent people in an act of revenge for what he thought was true love—a gift from God.

The moment Keane had stepped out the back door, Rutledge had called out to him to tell him that he had Sawyer and would kill him if he didn't retrieve Ashlyn from the house that instant. Keane had done his best to delay any reaction Rutledge might take in hopes that Calvert, Coen, or the authorities would finally make an appearance. Two of the three had finally been spotted, but neither Coen nor Calvert could enter the tree line without their target knowing. The question remained just how badly was Sawyer hurt and why hadn't he tried to communicate with them?

Rutledge had outplayed them all, all the while secretly listening in on their conversations to gain the upper hand. Having Parker come through the front door as a distraction was smart. It allowed Rutledge to engage each member of the opposition separately. What neither Keane nor Rutledge had been prepared for was Ashlyn's sudden appearance at the back of the garage distracting everyone. Pride and trepidation mingled, surging through him when Ashlyn finally stood up for herself. He understood what she was doing and lifted his weapon immediately, looking ahead off to his right and finally catching sight of Rutledge stepping forward in an angry response to Ashlyn's claim of contempt for his love.

Keane pulled the trigger at the same time Coen was able to get a shot off from his location on his left. The bullet that discharged from Rutledge's weapon hit the wooden structure behind him with a resounding thud, but Keane didn't move an inch as he fired his weapon one more time for good measure, aiming just above Rutledge's right ear.

Both Coen and Keane rushed forward, their instinctive nature having them disarm the suspect to ensure there was no more imminent danger from a body disconnected from its neural impulses. Andrew Rutledge lay face down in the wet grass, the rain drenching the back of his suit jacket as he jerked and twitched his last few seconds away. He'd apparently dressed for the occasion, not that he'd made much of an impression.

Keane leaned down and pressed two fingers to Rutledge's throat, confirming the lack of a heartbeat. There was no pulse…a few random beats followed by nothing at all. He quickly picked up the man's Ruger SR9C and then quickly turned to find Calvert helping Ashlyn up off the ground. The area became somewhat blinding as the electricity returned and lit up the backyard like a stadium full of overhead lights.

Ashlyn stood there shivering with drenched clothing. She'd never looked so beautiful and Keane would have gone straight to her had Coen not called out for help. Sawyer was lying on the ground just inside the tree line at the back of the property.

"He's breathing," Coen called out, running his hands over Sawyer's body and looking for any visible injuries. Sirens could now be heard in the distance. "I can't locate any wounds. Get an ambulance and—"

"No. No ambulance," Sawyer muttered, lifting a hand to his head and then rolling over to his side. "Shit, that hurt."

"Are you hit?" Keane asked, sharing a confused look with Coen as to what caused Sawyer to be unconscious for the half hour it had taken to secure the situation. "Did you take a knock to the head or something?"

"Electrocuted by that fucking generator," Sawyer mumbled as he finally lay back and put a hand to his chest. "That son of a bitch shot twenty-two thousand watts through my body. I know that stupid son of a bitch rigged it. He—"

"Is dead," Coen confirmed, sitting back against the wet ground and running a hand down his face in relief. "And you're not. I'd say SSI has successfully completed its first case through a series of completely lucky happenstances."

"I'd wager this protection detail wasn't technically supposed to end this way," Keane offered up, standing to hold out his hand to Ashlyn. That could be taken a lot of ways and it was apparent Ashlyn had gotten his true meaning. He pulled her to him, wrapping his arms around her while shaking Calvert's hand. "The situation wasn't completely in our favor."

"No, it wasn't," Calvert said, stepping over to where Rutledge's body was still laying, missing a chunk out of his head and a couple of holes through his chest. Keane didn't miss the raised eyebrow in regards to the way he was holding Ashlyn, but figured the man deserved to be kept in the dark for a while. After all, Calvert had purposefully sent him on this assignment knowing full well what kind of personal conflict had remained. "I'll call in the federal boys. I'll also call the Attorney General, seeing as how there's going to be a rather nasty amount of fallout considering Rutledge's position and the carnage left in his wake after our little gunfight this evening."

"Mr. Calvert?" Ashlyn called out, turning in a manner where she could still keep one arm around Keane's waist. "Thank you for trusting me."

Keane wasn't sure he wanted to know what Ashlyn meant by that, but his choice of inquiring about it was taken out of his hands when the police finally made an appearance. Calvert immediately calmed the situation down and let the cops know that they were federally licensed investigators, directing what the officers needed to do and the fact that they shouldn't contaminate the crime scene since it was a federal investigation. He went on to explain that the FBI would be arriving any minute.

Calvert did request an EMT for Sawyer, who was still protesting while eventually managing to sit up without going completely pale. The EMTs finally made an appearance and explained to Sawyer that many people who suffered severe electrical shocks could find themselves in trouble from what the laymen termed as dry land drowning, or pulmonary edema due to the aftereffects of the shock on the body. This could happen up to several hours later and they insisted that he spend the night in the local hospital.

"Man, you sure know how to get out of doing your end of the cleanup," Coen said, finally standing and trying to wipe away the grass that had remained on his jeans. It was useless and he finally gave up trying. "Next time, I'm the one who goes to check shit out and you clean up the equipment while I relax in the hospital."

"Your ass would have been fried, too," Sawyer replied, resting his elbows on his knees as he tried to recover his senses. He was damned lucky he could shake it off. "You asshole."

The two continued to exchange barbs back and forth as Keane led Ashlyn away from Rutledge's body. She'd had a hard time pulling her gaze away and he could only imagine the shock she'd felt upon discovering who had stalked her for so long, including murdering two of her colleagues. She was alive and safe, though. And that was all that really mattered.

"You scared the hell out of me when you came around that corner talking all that shit," Keane honestly admitted, pressing his lips against Ashlyn's forehead. He should be angry with her for putting herself in danger, but he was too relieved to feel anything else at the moment. "I was terrified that Rutledge would shoot you on the spot."

"I didn't know he'd gotten to that point," Ashlyn admitted, her cheek resting against his chest. He figured she was still watching the chaotic scene before them as Calvert continued to give instructions. "I truly thought he was still infatuated with me and that I could talk him down, but I didn't know it was Andrew. I can't believe I didn't see it, but I do remember what he was talking about. I remember what I said to trigger whatever mental break he had, but I swear it was an innocent comment."

"You don't have to convince me of that, Ash," Keane replied, knowing for a fact that Andrew Rutledge had lost his way from the pressure of having to be that promising prosecutor everyone spoke of. "Rutledge had a lot of people fooled, including himself."

"We were talking about our love of caramel one morning when he'd asked what I was drinking," Ashlyn admitted in somewhat of a whisper. Keane pulled her closer, if that were even possible, and allowed her to say what she needed to say. It was obvious she needed to share it with someone. "I told him a cinnamon caramel latte and Andrew said that he loved caramel. I joked that we must be soul mates. People say things like that all the time. It was such a casual comment that anyone would consider meaningless—just everyday conversation."

"Exactly," Keane agreed, pulling away far enough so that he could see her beautiful blue eyes. They were shining bright with tears and he wiped away the ones that escaped with his thumbs as he cradled her face. "You are completely innocent in all of this. You didn't make him do the things he did as a result. Andrew Rutledge committed these crimes, Ash. No one caused him to do anything. He decided what and how he was going to act toward the world because he was insane. You know how this works and you know the guilt you're feeling will fade with time."

Ashlyn nodded her understanding, but that didn't mean she wouldn't carry around some responsibility. It was just worthless remorse that would fade once she took the time to come to terms with what had happened. She lifted a hand and wiped away the raindrops that were now falling sporadically. The storm was passing and leaving a peaceful calm in its wake, along with a fresh smell in the air.

"I need to call Gina," Ashlyn said, resting her forehead on Keane's chest as she thought of all the things she had to do. "She can tell the team that...oh no!"

Ashlyn looked up and then at the house, causing Keane to realize that she must have left Parker locked away in the bathroom. He released her, but stayed close on her heels as she made her way through the back door the police had already opened, through the kitchen and into the living room. The house was now bright with light. She was calling Parker's name all the way, leaving footprints behind in her wake.

The bathroom door finally opened, Parker still clutching Ashlyn's weapon and flashlight in his hands. Keane figured it best to obtain the firearm first, considering the man's grip on the handle was a little too tight for comfort and his finger was a little too close to the trigger. Ashlyn proceeded to explain in detail what had happened and who had been responsible, the two of them consoling each other now that they could openly and honestly talk about what had taken place.

Keane stood by and watched, wondering where they went from here. They'd both confessed their love, though he would have certainly chosen a better time if one had presented itself. He wouldn't withdraw his declaration, because he'd meant every word of it. He truly wished his mother were alive to meet her future daughter-in-law, but he wouldn't tell Ashlyn that quite yet considering she wasn't aware of his plans to marry her as soon as possible. He'd lost her once. He wasn't about to lose her again to the fates.

"How did Rutledge know your location?" Calvert asked, walking through the front door. He was holding a phone to his ear and Keane assumed it was Coulter.

"He put a listening device in Ashlyn's pen…the one her father had been given upon his retirement, which had been handed down from him," Keane revealed, looking at the pen and knowing the feds would bag it as evidence. "Rutledge was tracking along with us every step of the way."

"The team worked well together," Calvert expressed after disconnecting his call. He crossed his arms and tilted his neck to the side, cracking whatever vertebrae needed relief. The black tattoo moved gracefully under the collar of his dress shirt, which Keane was noticing for the first time. D.C. tended to bring out the professional attire in those trying to impress, although Calvert's personality did that all on its own. "Royce is disappointed he didn't get more hands-on, but at this rate…I'm sure he'll get his chance."

"SSI specializes in protection details," Keane surmised, thinking of all the other cases they could be assigned. "I think my high-risk detail for the year is done, so I'll take the divorce case where simple, naked pictures are needed for proof of some affair and whatnot."

"Wait," Calvert instructed, shooting Keane a sideways glance. "I thought you wanted a thirty day probation. You still have another three weeks and some change left to that. We could use that time to see if you're really cut out to be an SSI agent."

"Seeing as you left it out of the contract," Keane stated with a smile, "I believe I'm now a full-time employee with great pay and full benefits."

Calvert nodded his agreement and then glanced at Ashlyn, who happened to be looking Keane's way. He would have to remember that Calvert liked to have the last word.

"And I have a feeling you're going to need it, Sanderson."

CHAPTER TWENTY-ONE

K EANE SLOWLY MANEUVERED his old Audi TT Coupe down
the gravel lane a couple of months after the case had been
resolved, giving Ashlyn time to appreciate the majesty of the
mature American Elms. Their abundant green leaves provided
more shade for the arrow-straight journey that would lead them
to the temporary headquarters of SSI, although he had a gut
feeling Calvert might actually make it a permanent move out to
the boonies.

"This is beautiful," Ashlyn said, admiring the view through
her oversized sunglasses she'd just purchased at the airport
because she'd forgotten her favorite ones back in D.C. They had
the windows rolled down and her right hand was currently out
the window, appearing to ride the imaginary waves of the wind.
One more trip to the big city to oversee the moving company
and she would be a permanent resident of sunny Central Florida.
He was just about to lace his fingers with hers when his phone
rang, this time connected through the Bluetooth on the stereo.
He glanced at the display and smiled. Sadie had a knack for
calling each and every time he drove down this lane. "Hi, Sadie.
Perfect timing as usual."

"Hi, big brother," Sadie replied over the multiple voices
talking in the background. "Hey, Dad is going to call you

because he thinks I'm being stubborn. And I just wanted you to know that I'm not."

"You are stubborn," Keane responded with a smile, taking Ashlyn's hand in his. He admired the diamond ring he'd inherited from his mother to give to his future wife. She would have been very happy with his choice, although maybe not so happy with Sadie's decision to buy their childhood home. "Dad was ready to let go, Sadie. You know that."

"I do, which is why I also purchased an RV for him and rolled it into the mortgage so he can go wherever his fancy takes him," Sadie declared, excitement brimming in the tone of her voice. Keane was already shaking his head at the confrontation he knew would come, but Ashlyn squeezed his hand to remind him he needed to take his sister's feelings into consideration. He sighed and continued to listen as Sadie told him her plans for breaking the news. "Dad doesn't know that and I don't want him to, so we need to say he won it in a raffle that the hospital was putting on for the orthopedic wing. We can say the biggest pain in the ass won it when they choose his ticket."

"Sadie, you can't lie to Dad, even if he is a pain in your behind." Keane couldn't believe his sister thought she could pull this off. He was starting to think that Calvert should have a remote Seattle office just so he could be there to put out the fires his sister created. "He's going to find out and then he's going to try and sell it, without ever having used it. Next thing you know, the local VA will be using it to ferry patients."

"That's not going to happen because I already sold him a raffle ticket, which is why he's being stubborn. I thought he should buy more, you know, to make it look legit. He only bought one." Sadie must have walked away from the group of people she was with to discuss her exploits in private. "Ashlyn, are you there? Can you please tell Keane that this will work?"

Ashlyn smiled and started talking to Sadie as Keane pulled the vehicle up to the main house, next to the garage. The smell of steaks being cooked over an open flame wafted from around the back of the house, causing Keane to practically salivate. He shifted into park and then gave Ashlyn time to finish up the call, very grateful that the two women in his life got along so well. He and Ashlyn had flown out to Seattle a month ago, with the sole purpose of her meeting his family. He'd already spent time with hers, even enjoying a rather nice glass of Pappy Van Winkle's Family Reserve twenty-three year in the retired judge's private chambers.

"Sadie, we'll back you up on this, but you should really just tell him the truth and say it's an early Christmas present," Ashlyn advised, taking off her sunglasses and leaving them in the console. The sun was setting and Keane already knew the sight it made as it set over the pond in Calvert's backyard. "We could even go half with you and say it's from all of us, if that will help."

Keane lifted an eyebrow, knowing exactly how much a state of the art RV cost. Ashlyn was trying to get him to loosen up the ridge in his wallet, but he'd been a saver most of his life. It was a little difficult to adjust to having someone else in his life to think about, causing him to believe he should have saved more. What happened when they had children? Raising a child or two certainly wasn't cheap. And college? Keane started to sweat just thinking about it.

"Hello? Anyone home?" Keane was surprised to see that Ashlyn had already disconnected the call and had apparently been calling his name a time or two. He shoved aside his worries and then opened his door, walking around to do the same with hers. He held out his hand and admired the navy blue and white sundress she had worn this evening. The fabric molded to her curves just right, as far as he was concerned. She stood and rested her warm hand against his face. "Are you all right?"

"Absolutely," Keane assured her, moving both of them to the side so that he could close the car door. He captured a kiss, not caring in the least if he smudged her lipstick. She laughed and immediately ran a finger underneath her lower lip to erase the smear. "You're about to be my wife, who happens to be starting a new job as one of the Orange County prosecuting attorneys. I'd say I'm doing more than all right."

Ashlyn had tried to include her team of paralegals in on the deal, but they all had moved on to bigger and better things in D.C. Mia had accepted a position with Bishop Vance. He'd finally managed to pull that one off. As for Parker and Reed, they found their own teams to complement. Gina replaced Ruth as the new Chief's executive assistant. Ruth found that teaching Pilates at Curves better suited her job prospects when she'd immediately retired from the D.C. office after Garner's death.

"You guys should just turn around and get a hotel room if you can't keep your hands off of each other," Brody yelled from the side of the house. He must have been making his way out of the garage when he'd spotted them. He stopped right before he was out of sight, lifting up his sunglasses to inspect Keane with a shake of his head. "I buy you a brand new wardrobe and you still show up in khakis with a stiff-assed pullover shirt. Ashlyn, when are you going to agree with my sense of fashion?"

"Never," Ashlyn called out with a laugh, grabbing Keane's hand and pulling him toward the loud conversation erupting from the back patio.

Sure enough, the entire group was lounging on the deck, overlooking the peaceful water. Calvert was standing before a large stainless steel grill, multiple steaks lined in a row with a dozen or more baked potatoes wrapped in aluminum foil on the top rack. Sawyer handed Keane a beer while Ashlyn gave him another kiss before joining the woman Royce had brought with him, although Keane was relatively certain the two weren't exclusive.

"Who's the blonde?" Keane asked, tilting the neck of the cold, clear bottle and taking his first sip of Newcastle Brown Ale for the evening. Damn, that was good. He motioned with his bottle to where the women were standing. "Royce, is that the same woman who was at the Orlando City game a couple of weeks ago?"

"No," Royce replied, stealing a chip out of Coen's hand before claiming the last lounger. Keane didn't mind. He leaned against the railing, calling out a greeting to Calvert, who was already charming the two ladies with his grilling skills. "That was Jenna. This is Meaghan."

The man was definitely a player, but Keane was relatively certain there was a reason for Royce's aversion to commitment. He wasn't as open as everyone else though. He was social, yet quiet…and those were the men with lethal secrets.

"Sawyer, can you go get me some plates?" Calvert called out, flipping the ribeyes over with the grilling tongs. The apron was a nice touch, but the white lace certainly didn't fit his personality. "Oh, and grab some silverware, too. We can eat out here tonight."

Sawyer stood and grabbed Coen's baseball cap before walking toward the sliding glass doors. He positioned it backwards, like Coen wore it, as he disappeared from view. Coen muttered some curse words and ran his fingers through his hair as Brody continued to talk about the new hardware he was receiving tomorrow and what it could do for them in the field.

They'd all been training these past two months, getting to know one another and how each of their skillsets could complement the other. There had been firing exercises, tactical maneuvers, and problem solving sessions. They had also reviewed the facts surrounding the last case ad nauseam. The most brutal had been the discovery of multiple dismembered female corpses in Andrew Rutledge's deep freezer in his D.C. apartment. Keane had spent the night just holding Ashlyn after that gruesome finding, coming to terms with the fact that she could have been added to that list.

It was also found that Rutledge had spent a good portion of his life studying Internet technology and that his second major in college had been computer science. His annual vacation usually coincided with the most recent release of Solaris Unix Operating Systems. His apartment was full to the brim with an amazingly complex server farm that baffled even the FBI's cyber department.

As it stood, Keane wouldn't be surprised in the least if Calvert gave them an assignment by the end of next week. The team had proven themselves efficient, capable, and deadly.

Keane was the first one to notice when Sawyer returned, although he was empty-handed. The concern written on his face said it all and soon everyone was turning to find out what was wrong.

"Townes, there's a problem. I was listening to the radio news you had on in the house about that approaching Hurricane Gilroy and..." Sawyer broke off, taking off the baseball cap and rubbing the back of his neck as he struggled with words. Keane set his beer down on the railing, already knowing this wasn't going to be good. "Shepherd Moss escaped from Union Correctional Institution in Raiford, Florida this afternoon. He's now on the FBI's Most Wanted list as of sixteen hundred hours today."

Keane and the others were clearly out of the loop, because

everyone was exchanging looks of concern. Who was Shepherd Moss and what was his connection to Calvert? The more Keane thought about it, the more he realized he *did* recognize the name.

"Moss?" Brody asked, lifting his legs up off of the lounger and setting the soles of his sandals on the deck. He lifted his sunglasses once more and set them on top of his head, studying Sawyer and then Calvert. "As in the serial killer who brutally murdered eighteen women?"

"Sawyer, could you please take over?"

Townes Calvert spoke so softly that even the usual rasp in his voice couldn't be heard. He quietly set down the tongs on the porcelain serving platter before methodically removing the apron, draping it over the nearest chair. He didn't make eye contact with anyone as he silently walked across the wooden deck and into the house, soundlessly closing the patio door behind him.

No one said a word, but all eyes were trained on Sawyer. What the hell had just happened? Keane reached out a hand when Ashlyn came to stand next to him, wrapping her arm around his waist in support. She leaned into him as they all waited for Sawyer to explain what had just taken place.

"What the hell, Sawyer?" Royce asked, mimicking Brody's posture as he sat up and rested his elbows on his knees. "Is there something we should know?"

"It's not my story to tell," Sawyer replied somewhat reticently, tossing Coen back his hat before walking over to turn down the burners. "What I can say is that we're about to have one hell of a mission hunting the most elusive serial killer in Florida's history."

Keane pulled Ashlyn to him, embracing her until her arms were wrapped around his neck. All he'd wanted was to deal with the simple divorce cases where he took a picture or two. When did those cases roll around? It didn't appear he was going to get that, but what he did have was someone to come home to every night. They'd come into each other's lives at the exact moment they needed each other.

An obsession might have taken a deadly turn, but it was the flames of desire and love that were left to be rekindled in the end.

The End

Books by Kennedy Layne

Surviving Ashes Series

Essential Beginnings (Surviving Ashes, Book One)
Hidden Ashes (Surviving Ashes, Book Two)
Buried Flames (Surviving Ashes, Book Three)

CSA Case Files Series

Captured Innocence (CSA Case Files 1)
Sinful Resurrection (CSA Case Files 2)
Renewed Faith (CSA Case Files 3)
Campaign of Desire (CSA Case Files 4)
Internal Temptation (CSA Case Files 5)
Radiant Surrender (CSA Case Files 6)
Redeem My Heart (CSA Case Files 7)

Red Starr Series

Starr's Awakening & Hearths of Fire (Red Starr, Book One)
Targets Entangled (Red Starr, Book Two)
Igniting Passion (Red Starr, Book Three)
Untold Devotion (Red Starr, Book Four)
Fulfilling Promises (Red Starr, Book Five)
Fated Identity (Red Starr, Book Six)

The Safeguard Series

Brutal Obsession (The Safeguard Series, Book One)
Faithful Addiction (The Safeguard Series, Book Two)

About the Author

First and foremost, I love life. I love that I'm a wife, mother, daughter, sister… and a writer.

I am one of the lucky women in this world who gets to do what makes them happy. As long as I have a cup of coffee (maybe two or three) and my laptop, the stories evolve themselves and I try to do them justice. I draw my inspiration from a retired Marine Master Sergeant that swept me off of my feet and has drawn me into a world that fulfills all of my deepest and darkest desires. Erotic romance, military men, intrigue, with a little bit of kinky chili pepper (his recipe), fill my head and there is nothing more satisfying than making the hero and heroine fulfill their destinies.

Thank you for having joined me on their journeys…

Email:
kennedylayneauthor@gmail.com

Facebook:
facebook.com/kennedy.layne.94

Twitter:
twitter.com/KennedyL_Author

Website:
www.kennedylayne.com

Newsletter:
www.kennedylayne.com/newsletter.html

CPSIA information can be obtained at www.ICGtesting.com
Printed in the USA
BVOW02s1142130716

455423BV00002B/41/P

9 781682 303641